CLAIMING WHAT'S MINE

JENNIFER SUCEVIC

Claiming What's Mine

Cover Design by Mary Ruth Baloy at MR Creations

Editing by Allison Walker Schorr

Home | Jennifer Sucevic or www.jennifersucevic.com

ALSO BY JENNIFER SUCEVIC

Campus Heartthrob

Campus Player

Confessions of a Heartbreaker

Crazy for You (80s short story)

Don't Leave

Friend Zoned

Hate to Love You

Heartless

If You Were Mine

Just Friends

King of Campus

King of Hawthorne Prep

Love to Hate You

One Night Stand

Protecting What's Mine

Queen of Hawthorne Prep

Stay

The Boy Next Door

The Breakup Plan

The Girl Next Door

PROLOGUE

Roman

Present

I'm beginning to lose myself.

I feel it happening more with the passing of each day, and it scares the shit out of me. During rare moments of self-reflection, doubt creeps in, and I question objectives that should be irrefutable.

For a man like me, this is a precarious situation.

Over the last three years, I've done everything in my power to keep her at a distance. I've been a bastard. I've been rude. I've tried ignoring her. I've withheld my friendship. Most days, I'm barely civil to her, because I know all hell will break loose once the floodgates open.

None of my tactics douse the spark that flares to life when we're in the same room. I'm a moth dancing too close to the twisting flames.

One of these days, I'm going to get burned.

Or end up with a bullet in my head.

A solitary image of her flickering through my brain is enough to make me grow unbearably hard.

I've found myself on the verge of reaching out to slide my fingers through the glossy strands of her dark hair too many times to count.

Because I'm a sick and twisted fuck, I often fantasize about wrapping the thick, rope-like length around my palm and pulling it taut. I want her lush, naked body bowing like a supple tree branch and bending to my will. I want her rendered incapable of doing anything other than submitting to my dominance.

The thought of her on bent knees, ass high in the air, cheek and chest pressed against the mattress as I hold her pinned, puts me on the brink of blowing my wad.

Sofia can't figure out why I act like such a bastard. I see the silent questions lingering in her eyes. If I were a lesser man, I'd fall to my knees and beg for absolution. But that's an impossibility.

I know the truth, even if she doesn't.

You'd think she would grow to despise me because of my churlish behavior. But she hasn't. Not yet. She may have learned to stay away from me, but she doesn't always abide by what she knows is best for her.

Sofia doesn't understand the feelings I stoke to life inside her. Nor does she understand the attraction vibrating in the air between us. But I do. I recognize it all too well. She wears her emotions across her heart-shaped face. And she doesn't realize that I feast upon them like a starved monster lurking in the darkness.

They're much too tempting for me to resist.

Something primitive inside me enjoys the way her body reacts to mine. Without meaning to, she displays her sexual desire for me. She flushes when our eyes meet. Her nipples harden under clothing. Her breath hitches, causing the pulse in her neck to beat erratically like the wings of a trapped bird.

I want nothing more than to claim her and make her mine.

But that will never happen.

Sofia Valentini will never belong to me.

I can't get her out of my head. I've tried losing myself in dozens of other women over the years. It isn't difficult to find a willing woman in this city. Not when you work for the Valentinis. Our reputation precedes us wherever we go.

And the pussy flows freely in response.

It makes no difference how high or low you rank in the organization. Name recognition is more than enough to get you whatever you want. These women want to live vicariously through you. Money, drugs, blood, and violence are powerful aphrodisiacs.

It's surprising how drawn some of these women are to a dangerous lifestyle. They want to singe their wings without getting burned. They want to dance close to the fire without getting torched.

But Sofia is different.

She's a princess who was born into this lifestyle, and now that she's free to make her own choices, she wants nothing to do with the Valentini empire. She would prefer to come from average, middle-class parents. Not one of the most well-known crime families in the United States, whose power and corruption dates back generations. And not one that resides in a multi-million-dollar compound on twenty sprawling acres of prime real estate along the shore of Lake Michigan.

Sofia Valentini is an exotic bird trapped in a gilded cage.

I've tried fucking women with the same olive-toned flesh. Big-breasted, generously-hipped, angelic-faced women I pretend with in dark rooms as I empty myself into their welcoming bodies.

But it's no use. No matter how hard I try, I can't forget that these women are nothing more than a poor substitute for the one I really want.

I've gone the other route, too, and screwed females who look nothing like her. Blondes. Redheads. Brunettes. Ones who are slim as reeds, with no tits to speak of. And ones who are tight and athletic and limber as hell.

You'd think a woman who strokes and plays with my balls as I slam into her from behind would be enough to make me forget Sofia.

It's not.

When Sofia should be the last thing occupying my mind, she pushes her way inside. Then I ejaculate in a blind outrage with a roar of frustration. Instead of providing relief, the release fuels the fury and lust boiling within me.

It also forces me to acknowledge and accept that I have no fucking control over my own thoughts, feelings, or body where Sofia is concerned, which pisses me off more than anything else. I take pride in being able to turn my emotions off as if they were a light switch. I couldn't do my job if I didn't have that kind of self-control.

But that capability is rendered useless with Sofia.

She's my weakness

While I might not be able to possess her, I'll be damned if another man lays claim to what's mine.

CHAPTER ONE

Sofia

Three years ago

"Well, hello there, handsome." My sister cranes her neck. "Who do we have here?"

At twenty-five, Francesca is already married and living in Philadelphia with her husband. I don't get to spend as much time with her as I'd like. Since we're two years apart, and she's my only sister out of four siblings, we're thick as thieves. I'm always excited when she comes home for a visit.

Our mother has arranged a shopping excursion on Michigan Avenue, along with two dinner parties with friends and family while Frankie's here. If there's time, we'll head up north to spend the weekend at our cottage in Door County, Wisconsin. Escaping the frenetic energy of the city is always a welcome change. I could spend days wandering around the quaint little towns dotting Lake Michigan's eastern shores. Like the family compound which lies north of Chicago, the cottage has been in our family for generations.

I don't bother glancing in the direction where Frankie's eyes are focused. I already know what—or who—has captured her attention. My skin prickled with awareness as soon as he stepped outside.

"That's Roman. He works for Papa," I tell her, ignoring the nerves dancing at the bottom of my belly.

Frankie snorts. "Of course, he does." Still staring at him, she states the obvious. "Damn, but he's hot."

The appreciative tone of her voice makes the edges of my lips curl into a smile. Clearing my throat, I admonish, "Have you forgotten that you're a married woman?"

Francesca and Dante have enjoyed marital bliss for two years, and Frankie is the happiest I've ever seen her. They were high school sweethearts and have known each other since they were children. I can't imagine my sister with anyone other than Dante, who has mastered the art of reining her in when necessary while allowing her to spread her wings and soar. Not an easy feat for any man. Frankie can be a handful. There's no doubt in my mind that the two of them were made for one another.

"Please." She rolls her eyes. "I can appreciate a good-looking male when I see one."

"Uh-huh," I tease, recalling how she threatens her husband with bodily harm whenever she catches him looking at other women. "Can Dante appreciate a good-looking female when he sees one as well?"

"Not if he enjoys having balls."

I burst into laughter. Francesca has nothing to worry about. Dante loves her beyond reason and would do anything for her.

How can I not envy them?

It's difficult to imagine having a relationship like theirs since my past is riddled with courtships that fizzled out around the six-month mark. Of course, being hung up on a man who wants nothing to do with me doesn't help my love life either.

Those thoughts viciously circle through my brain as my gaze settles on Roman. Looking deliciously sweaty, he makes his way into the yard from the basement gym where my father's men work out. I've unintentionally memorized his schedule. Every day like clockwork, Roman spends an hour lifting weights before taking a four-mile run along the trails bordering the wooded property.

I like watching him when he's unaware of my presence. Then I can look at him as much as I want without the fear of getting a glare in return.

I don't know why he doesn't like me.

But he doesn't. You'd have to be blind not to notice his disgust. He doesn't even try to hide it.

I sensed his disdain the first time we met. Each subsequent encounter has only intensified those feelings. I'm not sure what I did to cause this reaction in him, nor do I know how to alter his perception.

What I have learned in the time I've been acquainted with Roman is to give him a wide berth. And yet, knowing his feelings, I still gravitate to this spot at the same time every morning. I just can't help myself.

I must be a glutton for punishment, because I live for these fleeting glimpses of him. I file them away in the back of my mind to take out when I'm alone in my room.

Roman is one of my father's men. His disposition toward me shouldn't matter. But it does. I've racked my brain to come up with a rational explanation for his behavior, but can't find one. As much as it troubles me, I refuse to confront him and ask about it.

That would indicate I give a damn and that his opinion matters.

Which isn't the case.

All right, maybe it is.

I can pretend all I want to the outside world, but I can't lie to myself. I have a sick obsession with the man. I have no idea why he fascinates me.

No one would ever accuse Roman of having a sparkling personality. The man is surly to the extreme. At least toward me, he is. Every time he glowers at me, my breath catches, and my pulse runs rampant. My panties dampen whenever I imagine his big, rough hands stroking my naked body.

I'm not under any illusions that Roman would be a tender lover.

There doesn't seem to be a gentle bone in his body.

He's the strong, silent type, with eyes that constantly assess his surroundings to look for threats. I've never seen him kick back and relax. I'm not even sure if he knows how to smile.

His complexion is dark and swarthy. My guess is that he's of Italian descent. His body is hard. Strong. Honed for violence. A thin veneer of civility masks the explosive personality I sense lurking beneath the surface.

My sister and I silently watch as Roman moves through a series of stretches. I'm held prisoner by the sight of his muscles contracting and lengthening. Since he hasn't glanced in our direction, I assume he's unaware of us ogling him from the screened-in porch as we enjoy steaming mugs of coffee.

Roman's dark head angles toward us. His gaze collides with mine, and I realize that he's been aware of us the entire time. Our interest has not gone unnoticed.

The hairs on my arms rise as he stares at me.

"Well, well, well," Francesca murmurs, her voice full of amusement. "What do we have here?"

I try to look away, but can't. I'm transfixed by the sight of him. Other than the long black athletic shorts sitting loosely around lean hips, his sun-kissed skin is gloriously bare. His muscular chest glistens with perspiration in the early morning sunlight. His cheeks are flushed from his exertion in the gym. Dark stubble covers both chin and jawline.

This man is the epitome of tall, dark, and sinfully sexy. I'm not alone in my appreciation. I've seen the way other women watch him. He may not want it, but he attracts female attention without even trying.

My sister elbows me in the ribs. "Have you been holding out on me? Is there some kind of illicit flirtation going on between you and one of Papa's henchmen?"

Without acknowledging our presence, Roman severs eye contact and releases me from the captivity of his stare. Air rushes from my lungs, and my legs turn to jelly as he takes off at a fast clip toward the dense woods bordering the side of the property. I track him until he passes through the tree line.

I shake my head to clear it of the random thoughts that have accumulated. "Of course not. There's nothing going on between us."

"Are you *sure* about that?" she sing-songs teasingly, letting me know that I'm not fooling her for a minute.

Now that Roman has disappeared into the forest that comprises three-fourths of the property, my heart rate returns to normal and coherent thought floods through my brain.

"He can barely tolerate the sight of me, Frankie." The bitter truth of the words rings harshly in my ears and tastes bitter on my tongue.

Her brows pinch together. "Why do you say that?"

I shrug and murmur under my breath, "You saw the way he stared at me, right?"

"Yeah."

I glance at my sister. Our gazes catch and hold. We've always been adept at silently communicating with one another. It's a childhood trick that came in handy when we were trapped in a roomful of adults.

For the first time in my life, I don't want that mental connection with Frankie. If she looks too closely, she might see the feelings I have for Roman. And I'm not comfortable with owning up to something that scares and confuses me so much.

I casually wave a hand in the air. "He always looks at me that way. It's like he's angry that I'm breathing the same air as him."

"Hmm." She presses her lips together in a thoughtful manner. "Interesting."

None of my father's men have ever made me feel uncomfortable or unwelcome in my own home. But Roman does.

I console myself with the fact that school begins again in less than a month. I'll return to my apartment in the city, where I can immerse myself in classes and forget all about Roman Santori.

For a while.

I'm in my second year of a master's program in Educational Psychology. Most of the people I know who are my age don't spend their summer breaks living at home with their parents, but Mama and Papa are overprotective. They worry about my safety. We have an understanding. I stay at the compound during breaks in exchange for freedom during the academic year.

I really don't mind spending time at home.

Let me rephrase that—I never minded before Roman began working for my father.

I've been uneasy in his presence from the get-go. I've tried being polite and friendly. Not overly so, but enough to pass one another in the hallway or kitchen with a cordial greeting.

My attempts at civility were repeatedly met with cold, emotionless looks and a handful of muttered words that barely passed for conversation. I now go to great lengths to stay out of parts of the house I know he'll be in to avoid any more forced interaction.

As much as Roman intimidates me, I'm still drawn to him. His masculinity appeals to something infinitely female in me. My senses go haywire whenever he's in the vicinity. I don't understand my visceral reaction to him since he's the opposite type of guy I usually find attractive.

"I don't know," Frankie speculates, snapping me out of my musings. "I get the feeling there's more to it."

"You're crazy. I know when someone doesn't like me." My heart clenches as I add, "And for some reason, I rub this guy the wrong way."

······································

CHAPTER TWO

······································

Sofia

Two years ago

A hand settles on my shoulder. Startled, I spin around. As my gaze collides with Franco's, a big smile spreads across my face. A matching grin lights up his.

"Franco!"

"Long time, no see, Valentini!"

Without hesitation, I wrap my arms around his thin, wiry body and squeeze tight. He does the same. It's been at least a year since we've seen each other. Franco and I grew up together, and we've been close friends ever since. He moved to New York after college. We rarely get the chance to spend time together due to our busy schedules. Finding him here is a wonderful surprise.

"What are you doing here?"

"I was heading back from California when Pops asked me to stop home." He jerks his head toward the wing of the house where my father's office is located, his jovial expression sobering. "He's meeting with Enzo."

"And he brought you along for the ride, huh?" Trying to lighten the heaviness permeating the air, I joke, "Moving up in the world, I see."

He rolls his mocha-colored eyes and snickers. "Sure, I'll be running the show in two years, max."

I smirk as pleasure floods through me again at his unexpected presence. Regardless of the reason, I'm happy to see him. "I don't doubt it."

Like me, Franco has no interest in joining the family business. We've always had that in common. It's what bonded us together in the beginning. We're just two misfits who want to blaze our own trail in the world by choosing different paths for ourselves. Franco graduated with a degree in accounting. He's a whiz with finances. Unfortunately, his chosen area of study is a useful skill set to his father.

Mine, not so much. Which is fine with me.

"I was hoping we could get together while I'm in town. Are you free?" he asks.

"How about tonight?" I suggest, wanting to nail something down before we say goodbye.

"It'll have to be after eight; there are family obligations I have to take care of first. Maybe we can grab dinner and drinks and make a night of it?"

I pull Franco into my arms again. I've missed his friendship this past year. It's not the same with him gone. There aren't many people I can be honest with. Franco is one of the few. Even though I'm surrounded by family, friends, and my father's men, life at the compound is lonely.

You're never sure who can be trusted and who can be bought with enough money thrown in their direction. I've had supposed friends sell stories to the tabloids regarding my family. Once that happens, you grow cautious as to who you allow into your inner circle. When you do happen to find someone who proves themselves to be trustworthy, you hold on to them tightly with both hands because you understand just how precious a commodity it is.

I grin. "It'll be just like old times."

Still wrapped in Franco's arms, I feel *his* presence seconds before he clears his throat. There's no rational explanation for why my body is so finely attuned to his, but it is.

"Your father is wondering where you've disappeared to," Roman says to Franco in a clipped tone.

Franco tenses and turns to face him. When I try to step out of Franco's embrace, he stakes his claim by tightening his hold. The two men silently glare at each other as the atmosphere in the kitchen becomes oppressive.

Not once does Roman glance my way.

He never does.

To him, I am invisible.

It's been a year since Roman began working for my father and his dislike for me hasn't diminished. It's as if he made a snap decision and has never bothered to revise it.

Franco looks down at me with questioning eyes and tightens his hold. He must feel the tension permeating the air, too.

A muscle ticks in Roman's jaw, but his mask of indifference doesn't falter. He reminds me of a predator right before it strikes at prey. I can't imagine why he would lash out at Franco. They're not even acquainted with one another. Enzo and Franco's father formed an alliance decades ago. It would be foolish to create problems where none exist.

"I stopped to say hello to Sofia," Franco replies. "I'll be there shortly."

Roman's scowl deepens as he folds his arms across his wide chest. My eyes note the way his T-shirt stretches over every contour. His biceps bulge, muscles flexing with each movement. "Your father has grown impatient with your absence. Questions have surfaced that require your particular area of expertise."

Franco stiffens. He isn't happy about using his education in this manner, but he has a difficult time denying his father. His decision to distance himself from the family business has caused strife between them. I'm lucky in that regard. I have three older brothers and a handful of cousins to pick up that mantle.

Not so for Franco. He feels trapped in a lifestyle he neither asked for nor wanted.

"Fine." Looking irritated, Franco shoots me a glance. "I'll call you later, and we'll figure out a time and place. Sound good?"

I nod in acknowledgment. The warm comfort of Franco's arms vanishes from around me. Franco's eyes shift from Roman to me as if he's trying to figure out what's going on between us. He squeezes my fingers and strides through the arched doorway to head down the hall to my father's office.

My throat goes bone dry, and air leaks from my lungs as Roman frowns at me. I can tell the interaction we're about to have won't be pleasant. It's the *why* of the matter that eludes me. A surge of awareness zips through my body. My muscles tighten and lock up, rooting me in place.

I'm powerless to flee.

Powerless to do anything other than stare back at him.

How is he able to do this?

How does he tie my insides up in little knots with one hard-edged glare aimed in my direction?

I've never experienced this kind of intensity before. What a huge cosmic joke that the man who makes me feel this way wants nothing to do with me.

"You need to stop being such a distraction," Roman snaps.

The blood drains from my face. Confused by his reaction, I ask, "What are you talking about?"

"He's here for a reason, and you're getting in the way of it."

"Franco and I are friends. We were just saying hello."

"You're a distraction," he growls. "I don't think you know how to be anything other than that."

Before I can protest, he stalks out of the kitchen, leaving me to pull myself together after another disastrous conversation. But I can't. No matter how much I rack my brain, I'll never understand why Roman hates me.

CHAPTER THREE

Sofia

One year ago

I hiccup and clap a hand over my mouth.

I rarely drink, but the champagne went down far too easily tonight. I need to lie down upstairs until my head clears. My parents are entertaining guests from out of town, so sneaking away shouldn't be a problem with about fifty people in the house.

I grasp the railing to steady myself and climb the darkened staircase at the back of the house. During the early nineteen-hundreds, a large household staff employed by the Valentini family used this set of steps to move unobtrusively throughout the mansion. A shadow looms over me when I reach the second floor. Even though I can't make out his features, my body instinctively senses his presence.

Regardless of my feelings for Roman Santori, I'm fully aware of him on a physical level. It's always been this way and nothing—not his contempt, chilled demeanor, or indifference—has changed it.

My attraction to him feels pathological at times.

I've spent a lot of time trying to figure out and rationalize my strange obsession with him. Ironically, I'm in the last year of my graduate counseling program, and I'm unable to come to any rational conclusion as to why I can't move past my attraction for this man.

There's no logical explanation for it, which only makes my situation more unnerving.

I hastily step back, forgetting that I'm standing at the edge of the landing. Roman's hands wrap around my forearms and yank me forward until I crash into his body with my palms splayed across his solid chest. My hazy brain registers that his pecs are just as sculpted and chiseled as they appeared to be all the times I sneaked peeks at him during workouts. Before I can catch my breath, he spins us around so that I'm no longer in danger of tumbling down the stairs and shoves me away.

"Are you drunk?" he snarls, accusation and something I can't identify tinging his voice.

His misplaced anger scrapes at something inside me—the irrational part I keep buried deep down that has been foolishly begging for his attention.

Needing distance, I unsteadily step away from him. I came upstairs hoping to clear my head, and now it feels more muddled than ever. This is the effect Roman has on me. Every damn time. And I'm tired of it. Tired of wishing for something he's unwilling or incapable of giving me.

"Hardly," I mutter.

Even in the darkness, his contemptuous glare singes my flesh. "I think you are," he counters.

"Well, it really doesn't matter what you think, now does it?" I retort, enjoying my newfound bravado. I'm done with Roman's tight-fisted hold on me. I want to break free of it for once and for all.

He sucks in a sharp breath and releases it. "You're right, princess. What you do is of no consequence to me." Coldness fills his voice. His scorn could shatter me into a million jagged pieces.

I grind my teeth in aggravation.

I haven't been in his company for more than two minutes, and already my buzz has disappeared. I have no idea why he calls me "princess." I may be Enzo Valentini's youngest daughter, but I'm no pampered mafia princess by any stretch of the imagination. I don't live at the compound. I hold a job. And I don't take money from my parents. I suspect that he does it to piss me off, which makes no sense.

But, then again, nothing this man does makes the least bit of sense.

I whirl away without another word. All I want is to find my room and lay down for a bit. Roman isn't my father. Or my brother. Or my boyfriend.

His disapproval means nothing to me.

Well, it *should* mean nothing to me.

His hand shoots out and snakes around my wrist. I gasp as my back flattens against the wall and Roman's hard body presses against mine, trapping me in place.

"Do you understand that it's dangerous for a young woman to lower her guard by getting drunk?"

Of course, I understand that. I'm not an idiot.

If I were on a college campus or at rowdy downtown bar, I'd agree with him. A situation like that has the potential to end badly. I'm one of Enzo Valentini's daughters, which makes me a walking target for anyone with an axe to grind. It's one of the reasons I don't venture out much. Or drink.

"I'm in my own home," I quietly remind him. "I'm perfectly safe."

Fury flashes in his dark eyes. "Are you?" He snarls, the guttural sound setting off warning bells in my head. "There are men milling around, people who have been invited here tonight who you don't know. Any one of them could take advantage of the situation you now find yourself in."

My throat constricts as his words somersault through my head. I lift my chin. "None of them would dare to touch me." I can't imagine any of my father's men or friends laying a finger on me. Not if they want to keep theirs intact. Most just acknowledge my presence and carry on with their work.

His fingers manacle my wrists, yanking them above my head and shackling them to the wall.

My breath stutters as my eyes widen in shock. "Roman, what are you doing?"

I never say his name out loud.

I try not to even think it in my head.

The carefully controlled persona he normally exudes falls away.

"Teaching you a much-needed lesson, princess."

Before I can rein it in, a whimper escapes my lips. I don't know if it's because I want him to relinquish the punishing hold he has on me or if I want to push the boundaries to see what will happen next. It's no secret that I want Roman. I've dreamed about what his hands would feel like coasting over my body. I've longed for his lips to possess mine. I crave him on a physical level, no matter how menacing his behavior toward me is.

It's maddening.

Roman emits an animalistic growl and slams his mouth onto mine. His kiss is hard and rough like a violent storm devastating a rocky shoreline. Battering the landscape. Leaving havoc in its place. This is anger and frustration fused together in its most elemental and explosive form.

I realize that I'm consenting to forced submission by allowing him to exert his will on me. I should fight tooth and nail, rebelling against the firm grip he has on me.

But I don't.

How can I bring myself to push Roman away when I've craved this, *craved him*, for so long?

Those thoughts are so disturbing. I don't know what's wrong with me.

Growing up, my parents were loving and affectionate. There is no circle of abuse or violence that needs to be broken. Deep in the recesses of my mind, I know I shouldn't enjoy this rough treatment.

But I am. There's no denying the adrenaline-infused desire pumping wildly through my veins.

At twenty-six, I'm no virgin. I've had my fair share of boyfriends over the past seven years, but no one has ever manhandled me. No one has ever trapped me against a wall and held me captive while taking what he wanted.

Roman's mouth is harsh and demanding. I'd normally find this frightening, but I willingly open for him. His tongue invades my mouth, plundering the inside. It lashes and tangles with mine until everything in me clamors with frenzied need.

When I try to break free from the ironclad grip imprisoning my hands, he tightens his hold. His mouth leaves mine, blazing a hot trail across my chin and down my neck.

"I want to touch you," I murmur, baring my throat.

"No," he mutters, licking and sucking at my flesh. "You have no fucking idea what you're doing, do you?"

I'm not sure what the question means. Does he find me inexperienced or lacking sexually?

With a snarl, he releases me and moves away. I'm more dazed now than I was earlier from the alcohol. My mouth feels bruised and tender. Without thinking, I take a step toward him. I want the warmth of his hard body pinning mine against the wall again as his thick erection presses into my belly.

Knowing he wants me in that manner is a revelation.

"No!" he snaps, the harshness in his tone slicing through the mental fog clouding my better judgment.

His fingers wrap around my upper arm. He drags me down the dark hallway.

I stumble while trying to keep up with him as my heart thuds against my ribcage.

Before I can gather my scattered wits, we're standing at the threshold of my childhood bedroom. Holding me firmly in his viselike grip, he reaches out with his other hand and grabs the handle. He throws open the door and shoves me inside.

I stagger, catching myself before I fall. My head still spins from the alcohol and his drugging kisses. My eyes dart to the door in shock as he slams it shut, leaving me inside.

Alone.

I don't move a muscle as the last five minutes play out in my head. Did that really happen?

My fingers fly to my lips for confirmation. They're sore and swollen, which proves I didn't imagine anything.

If I'm smart, I'll avoid Roman like the plague.

But I'm not smart. I've already proven that time and time again.

CHAPTER FOUR

Sofia

Present

"Congratulations!" I pull Grace, my brother's fiancée, in for a hug. "I'm so happy for you two!"

My older brother, Matteo, has been popular with the opposite sex since he turned fifteen. An endless string of socialites and models have clung to his arm over the years. I don't remember seeing him with the same woman more than twice. I think my mother gave up on him ever falling in love. It didn't seem to be in his DNA.

But Grace changed that. I've never seen my brother so besotted. And it's easy to understand why. His new fiancée is kind and sweet. Her easy nature draws people in. I already love her like a sister.

Grace's smile widens. "Thank you!" She glances around the tent, which is filled with a hundred and fifty close friends and family. "It was so thoughtful of your parents to throw this party for us."

I pat her on the shoulder. "It's adorable the way you think you had a choice in the matter." Snorting, I shake my head. "My mother has so much more in the works for you. This little shindig is just the beginning of the circus that will roll into town.

You need to either jump on the bandwagon or get run over by it."

That statement would scare most women. Or at least make them rethink their decision. But not Grace. She's embraced our family as if we were her own and seems to enjoy how overly involved we can be at times.

If anyone deserves a storybook happy ending, it's this woman. Two and a half years ago, Grace lost both of her parents in a car accident. They'd been traveling in bad weather when they lost control of their vehicle. She doesn't have any siblings, aunts, uncles, or grandparents. It was always just the three of them. I've tried imagining what that would feel like—to be completely alone in the world—but can't fathom it. I've spent my entire life surrounded by family.

I have three brothers and a sister. There are dozens of cousins, aunts, and uncles in Chicago, New York, and Italy. Second and third cousins are considered family just as much as immediate ones. The Valentinis are a big, noisy, close-knit Italian family.

And I love it.

I can't imagine my life any other way. Everyone is always in each other's business. That's just the way it is. I can understand how it could be overwhelming if you aren't used to that kind of chaos. But Grace has thrown herself into the mix. It's amazing how well she fits in.

Since it's been a few years since Francesca got married and I'm as far from taking a walk down the aisle as you can get, Mama was over-joyed at the prospect of planning another wedding. Grace seems equally thrilled that my mother has commandeered the event.

"Did I mention that Teresa and I met with the wedding planner last week, just two days after Matteo proposed?" With shining eyes, she continues, "Can you believe he was able to squeeze us in on such short notice? Kenneth McKenzie is one of the most sought-after wedding planners in Chicago."

"Yeah, that sounds about right." I laugh at her naiveté. My mother was on the phone with Kenneth making tentative arrangements right after Matteo picked out Grace's ring. Mama is lucky that Grace is so easy going. Otherwise, they would end up butting heads.

"I'm so grateful that she's helping me with all this," she says softly.

"I'd be completely lost and wouldn't know where to start."

Her words tug at my heartstrings. Mama has been a strong force in my life. Wanting to offer comfort, I slip an arm around Grace. "I'm sorry. It must be difficult not having your mother here to help plan the wedding."

Grace smiles, but it doesn't reach her blue eyes. "It's been more than two years, and the loss of them still feels tender. I miss them the most at times like these." Lost in her own thoughts, she falls silent for a moment. "Your parents have been so kind and welcoming. I'm thankful for that." Putting on a brave face, Grace forces another smile. "It's impossible to be sad when I have so many wonderful new people filling my life."

Her gaze sweeps across the backyard, where a huge white tent has been erected for today's festivities. Space heaters are discreetly placed throughout the area in case the weather doesn't cooperate.

Thankfully, it has.

It might be late April, but you never know what you're going to get in the Midwest. The weather is unpredictable and often changes in the blink of an eye. It could be sunny and warm one day and snowy the next.

"And just look at this party!" Grace exclaims in an awed tone. "How did your mother pull all this together so quickly?"

"It's one of her many talents," I joke.

Sparkling crystal chandeliers hang from the tent's ceiling. Fifteen round tables filled with vasefuls of pink and white roses are arranged beneath them. Rectangular white-clothed tables line one of the sides, laden with meats, cheeses, breads, and pasta dishes that are kept warm in silver chafing dishes. Another table boasts a display of delicate desserts. I've been eyeing the tiramisu for at least an hour. Waiters in black tuxedos circulate throughout the space, armed with polished serving trays full of champagne. A string quartet tucked into a corner adds ambiance to the celebration.

I have to hand it to my mother. Once again, she's pulled off a perfect event. She's a mastermind at these kinds of affairs. She probably doesn't need Kenneth's help, but she adores him. My gaze lands on Mama, who's surrounded by a dozen or so guests. She has an infectious personality that attracts people to her like bees to honey. Even though this gathering isn't in her honor, she's in her element as mother of the groom.

Family from New York flew in for this occasion. Franco and his family also stopped by to extend their congratulations. I catch sight of my friend and wave. He smiles in return. I hope we can carve out a few hours to catch up before he leaves. With both of us working full-time and living in separate cities, we aren't able to spend as much time together.

As I continue studying the thick crowd, I'm jolted into awareness by dark, brooding eyes that are focused on me. The moment our gazes collide, a jolt of electricity shoots through my body, rendering me powerless to turn away.

No matter how many times I've tried desensitizing myself to Roman Santori's presence, my reaction is always swift and powerful. It's like the rest of the world falls away, leaving just the two of us.

Why him?

What is it about this man that attracts me like no other?

My fingers rise of their own accord and feather across my lips as our gazes stay locked from across the distance separating us. I've replayed that kiss on the staircase landing more than a thousand times in my head.

Over a year later, I still don't understand why he kissed me. No matter how much I secretly longed for a repeat performance, nothing has happened. If anything, Roman's become colder and more standoff-ish. I didn't think it was possible, but it is.

I keep hoping I'll outgrow my infatuation with Roman, but it hasn't happened yet. I'm beginning to wonder if it ever will, which sucks. I don't want to be hung up on a guy who can't even be pleasant when our paths cross.

When I meet new guys, I automatically compare them to Roman. The kiss we shared has ruined me for all other men. And it blew every other kiss I've experienced into oblivion.

If Roman intended to teach me a lesson, his attempt backfired spectacularly. Instead of driving me away, it's deepened my attraction to him.

I want him more now than ever before.

Grace clears her throat, and I realize that I'm still staring at Roman, who, along with my brothers, Giovanni, Matteo, and Niko, flank my father. Roman has become my father's right-hand man over the course of the last three years by making himself indispensable to the organization.

When I remain silent, she nudges me with her elbow. "So, Roman, huh?"

Heat suffuses my cheeks. This is one of those times when I'm glad I have olive-toned skin. A blush isn't nearly as noticeable as on someone with a creamy complexion. Like Grace, for instance. Matteo seems to take pride in bringing the color out in her fair cheeks.

I look away from Roman and scoff, "Of course not," wincing as the lie rolls off my tongue.

She arches an eyebrow. "Are you sure about that?"

I draw myself up to my full height. "I couldn't be more certain."

Grace and I have spent a lot of time getting to know one another during the six months she's been with Matteo. I've kept my feelings for Roman under strict lock and key even though we've grown close.

There's no point in mentioning them.

Roman isn't interested in me. He's done everything in his power to prove how inconsequential my existence is to him. After years of frigid looks and abrupt dismissals, it seems pathetic that I can't get over him and move on with my life.

"I don't know," Grace muses. "He looks awfully interested to me."

My gaze darts in his direction before I can stop it.

Thankfully, Matteo ends the conversation when he sneaks up behind Grace and wraps his arms around her.

My heart melts as I watch him pull her in for a backward hug. I'm happy that he's found a woman so perfectly suited to him.

When he nuzzles her ear, I pretend to gag.

Okay, maybe it's not pretend.

Their overly affectionate manner is enough to make anyone nauseous.

And jealous, too.

CHAPTER FIVE

Roman continually snags my attention throughout the afternoon even though I try my hardest to avoid staring at him. There isn't a moment when I'm not aware of every move he makes. My eyes track him everywhere he goes.

After dinner, Grace and Matteo open their gifts. I glimpse Roman exiting the tent as my brother holds up a silver picture frame for everyone to see. Acting on impulse, I head toward the house after him.

We haven't spoken a word to one another even though our gazes have connected several times throughout the afternoon. By unspoken agreement, we avoid interaction at all costs. Since that unexpected kiss took place, arm's length has grown to yards.

Roman moves fluidly through the thick crowd and slips out the back door. No one notices him except for me. I notice everything about him.

Pulling open the French door, I glance around the Tuscan-style kitchen with its dark cherry cabinets and sand-colored granite countertops. Roman is nowhere to be found. Instead of moving toward the living room, where guests are conversing in loud, exuberant voices, I turn toward the wing that houses my father's office as well as the security room that contains surveillance monitors for the entire property. I have a feeling that's where Roman's headed.

Moving away from the revelry, noise gives way to silence. As I approach Papa's office, I notice that the door is ajar, which is unusual because my father is paranoid about security and keeps it locked at all times.

I push open the door and peek around the corner, scanning the inside of the wood-paneled room. An antique mahogany desk sits prominently in the center. A massive fieldstone fireplace occupies the far end. Built-in bookshelves line the opposite wall, filled with old leather-bound volumes that Papa has been collecting since he was a child.

My father has a deep appreciation for the classics and has instilled the same in his children. I remember running my fingers over the worn spines before selecting a novel, eagerly devouring the words on each page, and then sitting down with him to discuss my thoughts. We would spend an entire evening in the matching leather chairs with a fire roaring in the grate, cups of hot cocoa and a bowl of buttery popcorn on the end table between us.

Those are some of my most cherished childhood memories of Papa. The best thing about them is that they have nothing to do with Enzo, the mafia crime boss. They're about a father and daughter bonding over their shared love of a well-told story.

Leaving the door open, I step into the empty room. The air is still, as if it hasn't been disturbed for some time. Roman may have turned down this hallway, but he didn't stop here.

Disappointment fills me, snapping me out of my daydream.

Oh my God, did I really follow Roman hoping to find him?

I blow out a long, slow breath.

I'm irritated with myself for not thinking about the ramifications of my actions and for following my instincts instead of using better judgment. I say a silent prayer of thanks that I didn't stumble across him. The muscles in my abdomen clench uncomfortably at the thought because he wouldn't have been happy to see me.

More like angry and irritated. Any conversation that would have taken place between us wouldn't have been pleasant.

I rub my temples in frustration. When am I going to get over this stupid infatuation and get on with my life? My feelings for him aren't healthy. I should rejoin the party and pretend this little lapse in judgment never happened.

"What are you doing in here?" a voice thunders.

I jump and whirl around, finding Roman looming in the doorway. His jaw looks like it's been carved from stone. The muscles of his body are coiled tight, as if he's on the cusp of attack.

All the thoughts circling madly around in my head flee. I gape in surprise as he studies me with hooded eyes.

He breaks the silence by biting out, "I asked what you're doing in here, Sofia."

Sofia.

The sound of my name sliding from his lips echoes in my head.

"I..." I trail off and clear my throat to give myself more time to come up with a believable excuse as to why I'm in Papa's office while he's outside entertaining guests.

I can't tell Roman that I came here searching for him. He won't like it. I don't want to imagine his response when he's already pissed.

Looking impatient, Roman arches a brow.

"My father asked me to retrieve a box of cigars from the humidor," I blurt, my palms damp with anxiety.

His stoic expression never wavers. I can't tell if he believes me or not. His steady gaze could burn holes through me. My heart hammers against my ribcage, the noise filling my ears in the deafening silence.

"Is that so?" he asks mockingly, making me wonder if he hears it, too.

"Yes." I swallow down the knot of apprehension in my throat and force myself to move toward the handcrafted wood and glass box in the corner. Opening the door, I select a box of Bolivar Belicosos. They're pricey, but not in comparison to some of the hand-rolled Montecristos in Papa's collection. "I believe these were the ones he asked for."

Not wanting to give Roman an opportunity to poke holes through my lie, I turn toward the door.

Roman doesn't move as I approach the exit. The closer I get, the harder I pray that he'll step aside. But he doesn't. His eyes stay locked on mine until I squirm with unease. The office is generous in size, but Roman's presence shrinks it, making it feel oppressive. As if there's not enough space for the pair of us to breathe.

I clear my throat again and summon strength, hoping it will make me appear unfazed. "I should really get these cigars to him." I internally flinch at how my voice came out as a husky whisper instead of its normal tone.

He shifts slightly but doesn't abandon his post. My fight or flight response kicks in as if I'm in imminent danger. I want to flee. I'm not a fighter. I never have been.

I'm ill-equipped to deal with whatever game Roman's playing. I don't have nearly enough weapons in my arsenal when it comes to him. I allow my instincts to take over every time. I always give in to the need pumping through my veins and end up hurt because he doesn't want me. He never has, and the sooner I realize it, the better off I'll be. It's time to stop the madness.

All I have to do is get out of here. Then I can hide the cigars in my room and replace them at a later time. The party should begin winding down soon. I can make the rounds quickly to say goodbye to everyone before taking off.

Gathering my courage, I shoot past Roman. As I do, he plucks the box of Bolivar Belicosos from my hand. I stop, staring at him in shock. "What are you doing?"

"I was on my way to see Enzo. I'll bring them out to him myself," he says with a smirk. "No need to trouble yourself, princess." His eyes stay locked on mine, the challenge glinting in them evident.

Ignoring the nickname that always manages to prick my temper, I swallow my panic. "No, he asked me to get them."

I make a swipe for the cigars, and he jerks them out of my reach. Anger stings my cheeks as I come away with nothing but air.

Goddamn it!

My mind spins. Clearly, Roman suspects that my father never asked for the cigars or he wouldn't bother with them.

Or me.

Desperate to get the box back, I inch closer. I'm tall, but there's no way for me to reach it unless I close the distance separating us. My body brushes against his, and he stills.

Roman's stance changes, his muscles bunching and tensing as if he's gone on high alert. His fingers lock around my wrist, and he pushes me away. "No."

The simple word cracks like thunder in the dark room.

I stiffen at the harshness in his voice.

A muscle ticks in his jaw. "I don't want you touching me."

Stung by the ugly words, my mouth falls open. I wrench my hand out of his grip and step away from him. He's not the only one who needs distance. Hurt floods through every fiber of my being. I fight back the tears filling my eyes.

My voice quivers as I hiss, "You're a bastard." It feels good to lash out at him. I want to inflict just as much damage on him as he's wreaked on me throughout the years.

Relief softens his carved features. "You're right," he agrees. "Whatever you do, princess, don't forget it."

Surprised by his spite, I spit, "I hate you."

Right now, I hate Roman more than I've ever hated anyone.

"Good."

With that, I run out of the room, my father's cigars forgotten. All the joy from celebrating my brother's engagement is gone.

When will I learn that Roman Santori is nothing more than a cold, heartless bastard? If I have any brains whatsoever, *this* will be the final straw. *This* will be the day I move on with my life and put Roman in the past where he belongs.

CHAPTER SIX

"Sofia, what's wrong?" My mother sets down the large platter she's holding on the kitchen island and takes a closer look at me. "Have you been crying?"

She's not aware of the feelings I have for Roman, nor do I want her to be. I feel like a fool after what happened in Papa's office. The last thing I want is her pity. It will make me feel worse.

I also know that if I tell her what happened with Roman, she'll have him fired immediately. Or worse. Roman has become a valuable asset to the organization over the years. My father heavily depends on him. My brothers assist Papa when needed, but none of them are interested in taking over when he decides to step down because they have their own business ventures to run. Causing problems for Roman will cause problems for my father if the person he wants to pass the reins to is no longer an option.

And I'm not interested in going there. Roman Santori isn't worth the effort, and part of me recognizes I'm somewhat at fault for what occurred.

"Of course not." I give my mother a quick hug and paste on a smile. It's forced, but it's the best I can muster under the circumstances. I just want to limp home and lick my wounds. I need to bury my feelings for Roman so deep inside me that they can never be unearthed. I hate that he ruined Grace and Matteo's engagement party for me. It should be a day of celebration. Instead, I'm hell-bent on escaping from my home and family as quickly as possible. "I wanted to say goodbye before I leave."

Her face falls. "But it's still early."

Biting my lip, I nod. "I know, and I'm sorry. I have some work to finish up for school tomorrow." Wanting to change the subject before she can pelt me with more questions, I add, "It was a lovely party, Mama. Grace and Matteo seem very happy."

The compliment does exactly what it's meant to. Her eyes light up as her frown morphs into a smile. "It was a beautiful party for a beautiful couple," she agrees. "Kenneth is a miracle worker. I don't know what I would do without that man. We're going to sit down early next week to start firming up the wedding plans. There is so much to do."

I roll my eyes. *Good Lord.* The idea of my mother putting her head together with Kenneth makes the corners of my lips twitch. Poor Grace. She has no idea what she's gotten herself into. If Francesca's over-the-top wedding was any indication, this one will be nothing short of a three-ring circus.

Better her than me.

"You did a wonderful job, Mama. Everyone had a fantastic time, and the food was delicious."

"Thank you." Reaching up, she strokes my cheek just like she used to when I was a child. It takes serious willpower not to close my eyes and sink into the comforting gesture. "You work too hard, darling."

I sigh.

This is a conversation she likes to sneak in at least once a month. I know exactly where it will end—with talk of wedding bells and babies.

"That's because I love my job," I remind her.

This is my second year working as a guidance counselor at Lincoln High School, which is located thirty minutes from my parents' house. Last spring, when I was offered a contract for the following academic year, I purchased a small bungalow in the same town as the school. Some people spend hours commuting every day. It takes me less than fifteen minutes from door to door.

The best part of my job is that I get to work with kids. It's reward-ing, and I feel like I'm making an impact on their lives most of the time.

It's also demanding. There are days when I'm overrun with students and meetings with teachers and parents, going in a million different directions before stumbling home blurry-eyed and exhausted. And there are afternoons when I stay late to finish up computer work and am too tired to make dinner for myself, choosing instead to eat a bowl of Grapenuts at the kitchen counter before falling into bed.

All that said, I enjoy it and can't imagine doing anything else.

"Yes, yes, yes." Mama waves a hand dismissively. "But there's more to life than work." She casts a knowing look from under thick, sooty eyelashes. It's one that says she expects grandbabies sooner rather than later. Since I'm not currently dating anyone, and haven't for some time, there's little chance of that happening.

Unless immaculate conception is an option.

Her words would roll off me like water off a duck's back any other day. But I'm not up for verbally sparring with her after my run-in with Roman. I still feel raw and tender. "I'm only twenty-six, Mama. There's plenty of time for that. I'm not in any rush." I mentally apologize to my sister before throwing her under the bus. "You already have one married daughter. Maybe you should have the grandbaby conversation with her."

According to Francesca, our mother badgers her around two o'clock every Sunday afternoon when they talk on the phone.

"Trust me on this, one day you'll blink, and you'll be out of time. You need to think about this now, while you're still young."

I'm tempted to roll my eyes but don't.

My parents are proud of me for earning bachelor's and master's degrees, but at the end of the day, they want to see me married to a nice, successful Italian man so I can settle down nearby and have three or four babies for them to spoil rotten. They may be progressive, but they're still old school at heart. Family is the pinnacle of everything. And that philosophy will never change.

"Didn't you mention a teacher at school who keeps asking you out?"

In a moment of weakness, I mentioned Drew to get her off my back. I probably shouldn't have.

He's a super-nice guy but...

It's difficult, if not impossible, to fall for another man when your brain is preoccupied with a churlish asshole.

I almost shake my head at that thought. I'm so aggravated with myself. This afternoon has opened my eyes to what an absolute idiot I've been. I spend all my time counseling students, sometimes teachers and parents, but it's obvious that I'm the one in need of intense therapy.

Or deprogramming.

Maybe an exorcism.

Whatever it takes to evict Roman from my head.

I should want to be with a nice guy. One who will treat me well. Not a brooding jerk.

Drew teaches chemistry and physics at Lincoln. He's one of the most popular teachers there. Students with no interest in science sign up for his classes. I have no idea how, but he breaks down challenging subject material and makes it easier for them to grasp. He has a great sense of humor and tries to infuse it into his lectures. I wish we had more teachers like Drew.

For obvious reasons, I haven't given in to Drew's pursuit of me. Maybe, in light of what occurred this afternoon, that's something I should reconsider. It seems shortsighted to turn down a great guy because I've been hung up on Roman.

"Mama..."

"Maybe you need to give this man a chance." Before I can utter another word, she follows up with, "Is he Italian?"

Smiling, I raise my brows and drawl, "Nooope."

Mama waves a hand as if that's a minor detail. "I'm sure he makes up for it with other redeeming qualities."

A grin tugs at the corners of my mouth.

Standing near the window that overlooks the sprawling yard, she nods toward the tent bursting at the seams with friends and family.

My gaze settles on Roman, who stands beside my father with the box of cigars he snatched from my hands.

"He's handsome, yes?" my mother muses, nudging my shoulder with hers.

I grit my teeth as Roman's hurtful words reverberate through my head.

I don't want you touching me!

Humiliation and anger slowly burn through me, heating my cheeks in the process. Channeling as much calmness and composure as possible, I shrug and say, "He's fine."

Unaware of the hurt pounding through me, Mama slyly continues, "I think he's quite handsome. Your father has given him a great deal of responsibility this past year. He's a strong man."

I refuse to discuss Roman with her. Ignoring her attempt to bait me into a conversation, I give her a quick kiss on the cheek. "Sorry, Mama, but I have to go. We'll talk soon, okay?"

Resigned that her scheming has been for naught, she sighs dramatically. "All right darling, but consider giving that teacher of yours a chance."

The woman is relentless.

And I wouldn't trade her for the world.

CHAPTER SEVEN

I smile at the student sitting across the desk from me.

Ella Michaels is eighteen years old and will graduate in less than two months. She's worked hard over the last four years and should end with close to a four-point GPA. She tested well on both the ACT and SAT, which she took at the end of her junior year, and had her choice of top-notch universities all over the country. Since she's a state champion swimmer who lettered freshman year and broke two school records in the four hundred breaststroke and freestyle, universities with D1 swim programs have vied for her attention since she was a sophomore. After visiting her top three schools last year and talking at length with the coaches, she settled on Florida State.

Intelligent, athletic, and talented, Ella is one of those students who make everything look effortless. She appears to have it all. It would be easy to hate her, but she's sweet, genuine, and goes out of her way to be friendly with everyone.

Two months ago, she came into my office in tears and told me she was pregnant. She was terrified to break the news to her parents. They were so proud of everything she'd accomplished. All she could see were her dreams and the future she had worked so hard to secure slipping through her fingers. We spent a couple of hours talking before calling her parents and inviting them to my office, where Ella broke the news.

They were shocked. It was painful to watch all the different emotions—distress, fear, anger, and sadness —flicker across their faces. I give them a lot of credit for not getting upset or flying off the handle. They both took deep breaths and agreed that it was disappointing, but not the end of the world.

Ella decided not to continue her competitive swim career at Florida State. She chose to stick closer to home so that she can commute to a local community college, where she'll begin taking classes next spring. Her boyfriend, Collin, also changed his plans. He'll attend the same college but will start right away in the fall.

This isn't how Ella anticipated ending her senior year, but she's embraced change and is doing what she can to succeed by adjusting her expectations and goals. I'm proud of how she's taken control of the situation.

I have a caseload of approximately four hundred students in grades nine through twelve. I meet with some kids on a regular basis. A few pop in almost daily. And some only require a quick check-in every few weeks to make sure they're on track and aren't falling behind. Others make weekly appointments during study hall to talk about the issues in their lives. Most of them are normal teenage growing pains.

Since the pregnancy came to light, I tend to meet with Ella on a weekly basis. She checks in and chats about how classes are going and how she's handling all the changes in her life. We try to troubleshoot challenges as they arise.

"Hi, Ella. How's it going?" Scanning her face, I notice a healthy glow on her cheeks. She appeared tired, drawn, and pale the past few weeks. My heart goes out to the eighteen-year-old because these last couple of months haven't been easy. "You look like you're feeling better."

At about four months along, you wouldn't realize Ella's pregnant unless you already knew. She's still quite slender. Morning sickness set in around the second month and she hasn't been able to keep much down. There were days when she had difficulty making it to school on time. She emailed me in the morning to let me know she was too nauseous to leave the house. I've done my best to run interference with teachers regarding her absences. Most have been flexible because they know Ella is a diligent, hardworking student.

While many students choose to take it easy their senior year, Ella challenged herself with two AP courses. Before the pregnancy, Ella didn't have any problems handling those classes along with the others in her course load—Spanish V, Anatomy, Literature, and Psychology. But now, she's struggling. Even though it broke her heart to stop training, she couldn't continue with such a rigorous schedule. It wasn't unheard of for Ella to spend twenty hours a week in the pool, often having two-a-day practices and dryland training. Without that, she has more time to dedicate to her studies.

And sleep.

She's been doing a lot of that lately as well.

"The morning sickness is getting better. My doctor prescribed some medicine last week, and that's helped a lot with the nausea."

"I can tell. You have more color in your cheeks."

"I'm still really tired, but at least I can keep my breakfast down in the morning." She cracks a wry grin.

"That's always a bonus. Are you having any trouble with your classes?" I try to stay preventative and nip problems in the bud before they get out of control. It's always easier to stay ahead of the train than be run over by it. "You're keeping up with homework and studying?" I know AP Calc and AP Physics have been a challenge for her. Both classes are college-level courses that require a great deal of work outside the classroom.

"Now that I'm not swimming, I have more time for studying." With a small smile, she muses, "I've swum almost every day since I was five years old. It's weird to have so much free time on my hands." Sadness creeps into her eyes. "I really miss it. A few days ago, I stopped by the pool and watched practice for about thirty minutes. It sucks not to be in the water."

"I know," I say softly, wanting to acknowledge her feelings. Change is difficult. Giving up something you love, or at least putting it on hold, isn't easy. "You can still get in the water and swim. As long as your doctor says it's okay, swimming is a great pregnancy exercise."

She shrugs. "It wouldn't be the same."

"No," I agree, "it wouldn't. But there's no reason you can't get back into competitive swim after the baby is born."

Her mouth trembles. "I know. My parents keep saying the same thing."

"I'm glad to hear that. Your mom and dad have been so supportive through all this."

She blows out a breath. "Yeah, my mom and dad have been the best. I thought they'd be angry after they found out about the baby. I imagined they'd kick me out of the house or..." she trails off. "I don't know, hate me or something." Ella shakes her head before continuing. "But that hasn't happened. They were just really disappointed that Collin and I weren't more careful about birth control."

I can only imagine what her parents are going through. To have your daughter all set to swim at the D1 level with a partial scholarship to pay for college and then have it disappear in the blink of an eye must be tough to stomach. Thankfully her parents are focused on the positives and have been wonderful about helping Ella through this pregnancy. Because Ella has such a strong support system, she'll be able to achieve anything she sets her mind to.

Ella glances at the digital clock hanging above my office door. "AP physics is about to start. I should probably get going. I don't want to miss anything."

Mrs. Schmidt, Ella's AP physics teacher, was a little prickly about making allowances for Ella in the beginning. She's an older educator who's set in her ways. She expects students who choose to take her class to dedicate themselves and be self-motivated. But she eventually came around because she saw how hard Ella is working.

Ella gives me a small wave and hurries out the door.

I sit back in my chair and take a long drink from my bottle of water, sighing because it's already one in the afternoon and I haven't had a chance to eat lunch.

There are two hours left before the final bell, and I still have a ton of schedules to plow through. As usual, the day is flying by. It's one of the things I love about this job. There's never a dull moment and every day is different.

I take a quick glance at my calendar. I have a student appointment scheduled in thirty minutes. Since it's quiet, I can use this time to check over grade reports. There are about a dozen students I'm keeping an eye on. I prefer to catch them before they get to the point of failing.

There's a soft rap on the door as I pull up the first student's file on my computer. A tall man with an easy smile fills the doorway.

Drew.

"I just finished lunch duty and thought I'd pop in to see if you were busy. I haven't been able to catch you in a couple of weeks," he says, leaning against the jamb.

Drew is a handsome guy with dark blond hair, green eyes, and sun-kissed skin. Looking at him makes me think of sun and surf. He's not from California but has surfer boy good looks. From conversations we've had in the past, I know he prefers spending his time outdoors hiking, fishing, golfing, and biking. Drew has an athletic build, which makes sense since he has an active lifestyle.

He's wearing khakis paired with a blue and white striped button-down. School employees are not allowed to wear jeans or T-shirts to work. The administration wants us to dress professionally.

From the gossip I've heard, several single female teachers in the building are actively trying to snag Drew's interest. Yet it's me who he continually seeks out. A few women have stopped by my office under the pretense of discussing student concerns before finally asking about my relationship status with him. I'm always adamant that we're just friends and colleagues.

Maybe Drew would like for there to be more, but at the moment, there isn't.

Whenever we're together, I compare Drew to one specific man. Even though Drew has a ton of amazing qualities, it's Roman who makes my pulse quicken. Which is beyond frustrating. There's nothing less productive than harboring feelings for someone who will never regard you in the same manner.

Just thinking about it makes me want to slam my forehead against my desk. How pathetic am I? It's not like I don't recognize the problem. Trust me, I'm totally aware of it. But I feel powerless to do anything to change it.

I smile and wave Drew into my office. "I'm glad you did."

He grins in response, looking boyishly handsome, and settles onto one of the chairs on the other side of my desk. "You must be overrun with students. Every time I drop by, your door is closed."

"The spring semester is always busy. I've been meeting with students over course conflicts in next year's schedule. It's eating up a lot of my time. There are so many loose ends to wrap up before graduation. Not to mention, I have two seniors who are touch-and-go right now."

He nods. "I'm sure it'll get busier before it winds down and then you'll have a well-deserved reprieve."

A few months of rest and relaxation sounds like heaven. As much as I love my job, it's nice to recharge my batteries before heading back to work in the fall. I've applied to take two graduate-level counseling courses at a local university over summer break and have been kicking around the idea of starting a PhD program. Eventually, I'd like to work in a private practice focusing on kids and teens.

Changing the subject, he asks, "How was your weekend? Did you do anything interesting?"

Roman's sharp features flash through my head. I almost grimace in response, but keep my smile in place. Sweeping him from my thoughts, I say, "My parents hosted an engagement party for my brother and his fiancée. A lot of family I don't get to see very often came. My sister flew in from Philadelphia, and other relatives came in from New York. I had a nice time reconnecting with everyone."

"Sounds fun. I didn't realize you have family in the area."

Again, Roman tries shoving his way in at the edges of my mind. I don't allow him to do it this time. Deciding to let Drew in a bit, I admit, "Yes, my parents and brothers are here in Chicago, along with some extended family.

Drew looks intrigued. "You've never mentioned them before."

He's right. I don't discuss my family with coworkers or friends.

"Oh, really?" I say casually. "Hmmm. I thought I had."

Drew has no idea who my family is. None of my colleagues do. I don't want them to know.

I adopted my mother's maiden name when I left home to attend a small private women's college in Wisconsin. It wasn't a decision I arrived at lightly. When I broached the topic with my parents, I was surprised by how quickly they jumped on board with the idea. My safety—the safety of all their children—has always been their top priority.

My father's biggest concern was not being able to surround me with the same level of protection I'd grown up with. The compound was heavily guarded at all times, and a driver escorted me to a nearby private school and anywhere else I needed to go.

Naturally, Papa tried strong-arming me into using security at school, but I quickly shot down the idea. The whole point in going away was to experience life by spreading my wings and enjoying the freedom I'd never gotten a chance to taste as a child. I wanted out of the small, protective bubble I'd been forced to grow up in.

Having guards on campus would draw too much attention. Which was exactly what I didn't want. For the first time in my life, I wanted anonymity. I wanted to be a normal college girl who lived in the dorms, studied at the library, and occasionally hit a party or two.

The moment I step foot on campus, I stopped being known as Sofia Valentini and became known as Sofia Bianchi. Four years later, when I moved back to Illinois and began graduate school, it seemed natural to keep using my new name.

When I introduce myself as Sofia Bianchi, no one judges me for being part of a notorious family. No fear or disapproval clouds their eyes. I'm also spared any star-struck looks and fake friendships from people who think knowing me will elevate their social status

I continue to hide my real identity because I love the life I've crafted for myself.

In an attempt to derail any more personal questions, I ask a few of my own. "What did you do this weekend?"

"Well, let's see, on Saturday, Grohl and I went hiking at the state park and then on Sunday, I did yard work before forcing myself to sit down and grade sixty-three physics tests. So, nothing too exciting."

Grohl is Drew's golden retriever and is named after Foo Fighters' Dave Grohl. Drew is a huge fan and has seen them in concert more than a dozen times. Grohl, the dog, appears to be a big fan of his namesake as well. He barks like crazy whenever Drew cranks up their music. I've seen the videos. They're hysterical.

"Ugh. That's a lot of papers to grade. I can't imagine how long it took."

"Roughly four hours. Most of the test was short-answer." A self-deprecating smile curves his lips. "I've been doing this long enough that you'd think I would've learned to make these tests true/false and multiple choice by now. Or Scantron. The short answer sections always kill me."

"I bet." I don't envy teachers, especially the ones in the English department. With all the essays students are mandated to write to meet state benchmarks and standards, they're always lugging home briefcases full of papers. "At least you were able to spend some time outside. It was a great weekend. The weather was beautiful."

"It really was. Sunny and in the seventies. Can't beat that. Hiking always clears my head. You ever been?"

"Only once. My college roommate talked me into hiking a nearby trail and that, unfortunately, turned out to be a traumatic experience. We somehow ended up on the wrong path and were lost for half the day. Thankfully, a ranger found us before it started getting dark out. I had images of getting eaten by a grizzly bear. I don't think we ever stopped blowing our whistles." The memory makes me smile. It wasn't funny at the time, but I laugh about it now.

"Where were you hiking? Out West?"

I laugh and shake my head. "No, why?"

"Montana, Wyoming, and Idaho are the only places in the lower forty-eight where you'll find grizzlies." He shrugs. "I think there might even be a few in Washington."

"Rational thought wasn't exactly prevalent out in the middle of nowhere. By the time the ranger found us, we were both hysterical."

He chuckles. "You're right, that does sound traumatic."

"It was," I say cheerfully. "Needless to say, I haven't been hiking since."

"Maybe what you need is a more experienced guide. Someone who knows what they're doing and can keep you safe."

I smile, turning the idea over in my head. "Maybe."

He shifts his body toward me. The air in the office changes subtly. My breath catches at the back of my throat as I wait to see what will happen next.

"So, I was wondering if maybe you'd like to get together this weekend. I promise we won't go hiking." His eyes twinkle with humor. "At least not this time."

I laugh at his joke and the tension that had permeated the air dissolves.

Looking encouraged by my response, he continues. "We can get together during the day if that would make you more comfortable. Just think of it as two friends meeting up to have— "

"Okay."

His eyes widen almost comically, and he leans in closer, cocking his head. "I'm sorry, can you go back and rewind that last part? Did you just agree to go out with me after almost a year of shooting me down?"

I wince as another gurgle of laughter escapes.

Is that what I've just done?

Did I agree to go on a date with Drew?

I sit up straighter. "Yeah, I guess I did."

Grinning, he pumps a fist in the air like an excited kid. "Yes! See? Persistence really does pay off."

His response makes me laugh harder, and you know what? It feels good. *Really good*. This light-hearted exchange is nothing like the ones I've experienced with—

No.

I refuse to go there.

He's the last person I want to dwell on. Or let ruin this moment. I've permitted Roman to steal three years of my life, and I won't allow it to continue any longer. I'm done. What's happening right now is the beginning of me moving on with my life. It's been a long time coming. I should have done this years ago. In order to get over Roman, I have to give other men a chance.

Drew is the perfect guy to move on with. He's intelligent, funny, handsome, and kind. He has all the qualities I'm looking for in a partner, and I know he's interested in me. While I don't have romantic feelings for him at the moment, who's to say they won't develop over time?

I'll never know if I don't try.

The bell rings, signaling a five-minute break before the start of sixth period.

Drew stands. "I'd better head to class, but we'll talk later to firm up plans for the weekend."

I nod. A few butterflies wing to life in my belly. I'm really doing this. I agreed to go out with Drew. "That sounds good."

"No," he shoots me a bright smile along with a wink, "It sounds fantastic."

Those words settle the jangled nerves buzzing around inside me. He's right— it does sound fantastic. We're going to have a great time.

And who knows?

Maybe this is the beginning of an amazing relationship.

CHAPTER EIGHT

Drew picks me up at my house at six o'clock.

He offers me a stunning bouquet of wildflowers after I open the door. Burying my nose in the blooms, I invite him in and arrange them in a vase, adding *thoughtful* to Drew's list of admirable qualities.

We head downtown to have dinner at a popular steakhouse he's secured reservations at. Within the first five minutes in the car, we banter back and forth, cracking jokes and laughing. My concerns about not having enough to discuss over the course of the evening seem unwarranted.

There's nothing awkward or stilted about being in his company.

Which is a huge relief.

As a colleague, I immediately liked Drew. He has a laid-back, affable manner that instantly puts people at ease. And he's knowledgeable and interested in a wide variety of subjects. From politics to musical choices, we run the conversational gamut during the drive.

We share a bottle of white wine over dinner. The two glasses I consume don't make me feel intoxicated, just light and happy. After repeatedly turning him down and shying away from involvement, I'm glad I agreed to go out with him. I want to kick myself for not doing it sooner because I'm having the best time.

I'm even toying with the idea of inviting him back to my house at the end of the evening. Not to spend the night, of course. I have no intention of moving *that* fast. Especially with someone I have to see at work the following Monday.

Maybe kissing Drew will help move things along in the attraction department. It can't hurt, right? I like him and think he's good-looking. But there isn't a spark. Not yet. I hope that will develop with more time.

I offer to split the check for the meal, but he insists on taking care of it himself. Dinner was wonderful and the company even more so. I don't think I've ever had a nicer time on a first date.

As we leave the restaurant, Drew says, "I thought we could check out a club a few blocks from here. You game?"

The evening has been a huge success. I'm not ready for it to be over with yet, so…

Why not? Is there a reason I shouldn't go out and have fun with Drew?

Nope. I can't think of one.

"Yeah, that sounds great. Let's do it."

When was the last time I cut loose and danced at a club?

I can't remember. It's been *that* long.

I'm twenty-six, but I've never really been into the club or bar scene. I'm more of a homebody. I enjoy snuggling up with a good book on a Saturday night and listening to music while recuperating from the work week before gearing up for the start of another.

Drew nods at the stop light half a block away. "It should be right around the corner."

I'm not surprised to see tons of people on the sidewalk. They come downtown for the restaurants, museums, shopping, bars, and clubs. An irrepressible energy hums on the streets that is unlike anywhere else. I love this area. It makes me doubly glad that I gave in and agreed to this date.

Even though it's May, and the temperature reaches the seventies during the day, the nights are still chilly. I tighten my light jacket, trying to ward off the cold. Drew wraps an arm around me and pulls me closer, shielding me from the wind. I tense and wait for discomfort to set in. But it doesn't. The intimacy between us feels natural. Muscles loosening, I lean into him. His masculine scent—a cross between the fresh outdoors and sunshine—assaults my senses.

As we turn the corner, I catch a glimpse of the red brick building we're heading toward and nearly stumble. I'd been so focused on what a great time we were having that I hadn't given much thought to the club he was interested in checking out. Perhaps I should have.

Drew stops and eyes the long line of people snaking around the corner. "Wow," he mutters, disappointment coloring his voice. "I didn't expect such a huge crowd."

The crowd doesn't surprise me at all. Covet quickly made a name for itself as one of Chicago's premier hot spots for people under thirty when its doors opened two years ago.

I shift my attention to Drew. "I didn't realize you were talking about Covet." Muscles twitch in my belly as nervousness sets in.

His brows pinch together. "Yeah, a friend went here a few weeks ago and said it was amazing. I'd like to see if he's right, but that line is too long. I doubt half these people will make it inside by closing time."

There must be at least two hundred people waiting for a chance to walk through the doors. It's an upscale crowd. Men are dressed in suits. Women wear short skirts and slinky dresses paired with sky-high heels.

We walk toward the unassuming entrance, where a bouncer stands guard in front of a red velvet rope. One or two people trickle out of the club, but he doesn't allow anyone inside. He's a mountain of a man with thickly corded arms folded across a tight black T-shirt that's molded against his broad chest.

Our pace slows as Drew studies the line again. "I really don't want to spend the rest of the night waiting outside a club we have zero chance of getting into."

I make a snap decision and say, "Maybe you should ask someone near the end if they've moved at all. It'll give us a better idea of what's going on."

"Really? Are you sure?" He looks surprised by my suggestion. "Because it's not a big deal. We don't have to stay. There are plenty of other bars in the area."

I give him a reassuring smile. "We might as well check this place out since we're already here."

He glances at the crowd and frowns. "You'll be okay here by yourself?"

"Yeah, I'll stick close to the bouncer. Don't worry, I'll be fine." Drew has no idea just how safe I am. "But, thank you," I add because his concern is sweet, and I genuinely appreciate it.

Still looking hesitant, he nods. "All right, I'll be gone two minutes, tops."

"I won't move." As soon as Drew disappears around the corner, I make my way to the bouncer and smile. "Hi, Lucas."

He straightens to his full height when he recognizes me. At six foot four and two hundred and fifty pounds, Lucas is a big dude. There aren't many people who want to mess with him. Which is exactly why my brother hired him. "Hey, Ms. Bianchi," he replies. "How you doing tonight?"

"I'm good." I glance down the block, making sure there's no sign of Drew. He seemed nervous about leaving me alone, so I need to work fast. "Any chance we can skip the line?"

With sausage-like fingers, he slides his shades down the bridge of his nose until light blue eyes meet mine. "Are you serious? The boss would have my ass if I didn't usher you inside pronto." He leans in and says, "He'd have my head right now if he knew you were standing out on the street by yourself." Brows drawing together, he twists his thick neck from side to side. "You here with someone, Ms. B?"

I want to roll my eyes but don't because Lucas is just following orders. All three of my brothers are overprotective when it comes to me and Frankie.

"Yep. He'll be right back." I pause and lower my voice. "Would you do me a favor, Lucas?"

The edges of his lips curl into a grin. "Whatever you need, consider it done."

"When the man I'm with returns, would you pull him aside and tell him that you'll let us inside the club?" I nip my bottom lip and add, "And could you pretend that we don't know each other?"

"You got it." Lucas immediately answers. My brother's staff is well-trained. I'm sure my odd request raised questions in his mind, but he knows better than to ask them.

"Thanks." I sneak another peek to look for Drew. "Is Matteo here?"

"Nope. The boss left about thirty minutes ago."

All of my muscles relax. "Okay, good."

I love my brother, but I'm not ready to introduce him to Drew. Nor am I ready to explain how I know Matteo Valentini. Most people don't realize that a Valentini owns Covet. Not wanting his club associated with the family business, my brother tries to keep the two separated.

Had I realized earlier that Drew wanted to check this place out, I would have steered us in a different direction. But it's too late. As long as Matteo isn't around, I can move anonymously through the club. No one will notice me.

As I step away from Lucas, Drew reappears and makes his way over to me. "Hey, everything, okay?"

"Of course." I smile, feeling more at ease about the situation. "Perfectly fine." I nod at the line. "How does it look? Think we have a shot at getting in?"

He shakes his head and sighs. "I don't think so. I talked to a guy who's been waiting for two hours already. He said the line has barely moved."

"Really?"

"Yeah. I don't want to spend our first date standing around, waiting in line. That's no fun. Let's find another bar. We'll grab a drink and talk. I noticed one by the restaurant."

"Hey, buddy!" a deep voice yells.

We look at Lucas, and Drew whispers, "Is he talking to me?"

I suppress my smile at the dubious expression on Drew's face. "Seems like it."

Lucas jerks his head when Drew doesn't move. "Yeah, you! Come here."

"Hmm. Okay, I guess I'll go see what this is about. I'll be right back." He mutters out the side of his mouth, "I hope."

"Okay." The corners of my lips twitch as I watch Drew cautiously approach Lucas. Less than thirty seconds later, Drew returns with a bewildered look on his face. "The bouncer says we can go inside."

"Really?" I feign surprise. "How come?"

Drew shrugs. "Honestly, I don't have a clue. I wasn't about to argue with him." He jokes, "Have you taken a good look at that guy? He could flatten me with one swing of his fist. Which, if you haven't noticed, looks to be the size of Thor's hammer. Whatever he said, I agreed with."

Lucas may look intimidating with his height and stocky build, and he certainly knows how to take care of business when required, but he isn't big on unnecessary violence. I squeeze Drew's bicep. "I'm willing to bet that you could hold your own."

His brows rise. "Against him?" He shakes his head. "I don't think so, but thanks for your vote of confidence." With a smile, he jerks his head at the entrance. "You ready to do this?"

I take a deep breath. I'm as ready as I'll ever be. As long as no one recognizes me, everything will be just fine. "Yup."

Drew slips my fingers into his hand. Lucas unsnaps the rope and lets us pass, telling us to have a good time. I leave my jacket and purse with the attendant at the coat check in the vestibule.

Walking into Covet is like falling down the rabbit hole. It's an over-the-top sensory overload extravaganza. People often pause and try to take in everything at once with wide eyes because there's so much going on.

The club is three stories tall. A massive dance floor that lights up occupies most of the main level. A long glass bar sits at the far end. Every kind of high-end liquor is displayed on thin crystal shelves. Matteo stocks most of the well-known brands along with rare ones, including thousand-dollar bottles of Absolut Crystal and twenty-five thousand-dollar bottles of Legacy by Angostura.

On the second and third floors, balconies wrap around the perimeter of the dance space so patrons can watch the spectacle below. A DJ spins records in an elevated booth. Fog creeps across the ground and strobe lights with different colors bounce over the walls in the darkened club. Girls twist their bodies around poles on platforms strategically placed throughout the first story.

All of the dancers and bartenders who work at Covet are female. Their bodies are spray-painted to look like they're wearing matching swimsuits or lingerie. I've also seen them decorated with flowers blooming across their toned flesh. The end result is stunning. I give these women a lot of credit for walking around in nothing more than a coat of paint and a smile.

"Mike told me this place was crazy," Drew yells over the pumping beat of the music. "He was right."

Without a doubt, Covet *is* crazy. But it's a cool, addictive kind of crazy. I can't stop myself from giggling because I can tell Drew's a little stunned by the wonderland surrounding him.

"Do you want to grab a drink first or hit the dance floor?"

I glance at the space packed with writhing bodies, surprised by the longing filling me. "Let's dance for a bit, then we can get a drink."

"Sounds good."

He tows me through the crush of gyrating people until we carve out a small space for ourselves. I have no idea how long Drew and I dance. After a song or two, my mind shuts off, and I don't think about anything other than the deep bass resonating throughout my bones and settling in the pit of my stomach. I lose myself in the music and people moving around us.

Drew leans toward me. "Do you want to take a breather and grab something to drink?"

Coming back into myself, I nod. A cold bottle of water sounds like heaven right now.

Keeping my hand firmly ensconced in his, Drew navigates through the thick crowd toward the bar. In most places, it's two or three people deep.

I decide to freshen up to avoid being recognized. Since I helped interview most of the bartenders when the club first opened, there's a good chance of that happening. Standing on tiptoe so he can hear me better, I say, "I'll be right back. I'm going to the restroom."

He nods. "I'll be here." As I walk away, he asks, "What should I get for you?"

"A bottle of water would be great," I call back. "Thanks!"

It takes a couple of minutes to reach the ladies' room, and like I expected, there's a long line. Instead of waiting, I head toward the staff restroom located through a pair of doors marked *Employees Only* in bold black letters.

The music and noise fade right after the doors close behind me. This area is deserted. When it's this crowded on a Saturday night, it's difficult for anyone working the floor to get away for a break.

My footsteps echo off the glazed concrete floor as I walk toward the bathroom tucked around the corner. Flipping the switch, light illuminates the chrome and glass space. Just as I close the door, masculine fingers wrap around the wood, catching it.

I gasp, caught off guard by the unexpected intrusion. A scream gathers in my throat as the door is forced open and my eyes collide with dark ones.

CHAPTER NINE

"What are you doing?" I rasp.

Roman slips inside the bathroom and shuts the door behind him.

The sound of the lock clicking into place is like a gunshot in the small room. My heart pounds in my chest. I want to run away, but I'm not sure if I can move my legs.

"Why are you here?" he fires back.

I jerk in response. "Excuse me?"

"You heard me," he retorts in a gruffer tone. "Why are you here?"

My shoulders straighten as anger roils through me. Who the hell does this man think he is? I don't owe him any explanations. Roman Santori works for my father. Not the other way around. And he certainly isn't my keeper.

"I'm here with a," I pause, debating if I should say *friend* or *date*. Screw it, I'm not going to hide what I'm doing. "Date."

He steps toward me, and I reflexively back away to keep the same amount of distance between us.

I take a deep breath and force it out, trying to settle my jangled nerves. Being this close to Roman always sends my pulse skyrocketing. I need a distraction, or I'll fall to pieces.

Ignoring Roman, I turn to the mirror above the sink to inspect myself. My hair is a mess. I finger-comb it, struggling to steady my shaky fingers. As I finish smoothing the long strands into place, he comes up behind me and aligns our bodies. My muscles lock in response.

Our gazes meet in the looking glass. Fury blazes in his eyes.

Run!

The desperate warning flashes through my brain like a bright neon sign. I have to get out of here. I need to get away from him before something catastrophic happens.

He presses his hard body into mine, caging me between him and the sink. I gulp and try to angle myself as far from him as possible.

"What do you want?" I ask, embarrassed by how my voice trembles as much as my body.

"Who is he?" Roman rasps against the shell of my ear.

A shiver zips down my spine as his gaze pierces mine in the silvery glass. Held captive, I'm powerless to look away. My insides pitch and roll from the intimate way he's positioned against me.

I want to lean back, close my eyes, and bask in the feel of his strong hands holding me against the unrelenting steel of his sculpted body. But I know Roman will crush my heart without a second thought if I give him any more of myself, so I snap, "That's none of your business."

Placing a hand on each hipbone, he jerks me back until nothing separates us but a few thin layers of clothing. His thick erection juts into my backside. I bite my lip to stifle a groan as thick spurts of pleasure flood through me.

My brain screams at me to fight and get out of his grasp, but the way his fingers possessively bite into my flesh feels way too good. If this were any other man, I would knee him in the balls while screaming my head off.

But this isn't any other man. *It's Roman.* The man I've desired for years.

Deep down, I know he isn't forcing contact. If I wanted, *truly wanted*, to break free, I could. I could bolt straight from Roman into Drew's waiting arms. As that bit of truth sinks in, everything swirling madly inside me deflates.

Because therein lie the problem.

When it comes down to it, I have no desire to escape.

No matter how much I want to pretend that I'm moving on and my feelings have diminished, attraction continues to pump wildly through me. I've given it time to run its course and prayed for it to go away, but it never does. Instead of dissipating, it gains strength. I want Roman more than I did in the beginning.

That realization makes me want to crumple into a small ball.

I'm never going to get over him.

"It feels very much like my business," he whispers, dragging his lips over my ear.

I shake my head. "Nothing I do is your business." Angry for being toyed with, I turn in his arms and use all my strength to shove at his chest.

In a lightning-quick movement, he spins me around until my spine aligns with his chest again. He pins me in place by resting a hand on my collarbone. His other hand plows into my hair and grabs a fistful of strands, pulling them taut until my head drags back and my chin tips up at the ceiling.

My heart thumps frantically as panic sets in. I look in his eyes in the mirror and ask, "Why are you doing this?"

His lips meet my ear again. His warm breath spills onto the delicate flesh, filling me with warmth and weighing my eyelids as lust careens through me. "I wish I knew."

My belly spasms in response to the disgust filling his voice. "Then let me go," I say, hoping he releases me for both of our sakes.

"I can't," he grates out, running the tip of his nose along the column of my throat.

I swallow hard while processing our strange intimacy. This rough treatment should repulse me, but it doesn't. It has the opposite effect. I want to revel in his breath sweeping over my skin and the punishing grip he has on my hair. The way Roman takes what he wants turns me on. It fulfills a need buried deep inside me. One I'm afraid to inspect too closely.

Breaking into my thoughts, he muses, "Do you know how long I've imagined wrapping your hair around my fist?" He emphasizes the softly spoken words with a slight tug.

A whimper of pleasure slips free as electricity bolts through me.

He swears under his breath. "Do you like that?"

I press my lips together to stop any more sounds from escaping. Thoughts and feelings wage war in me for relishing his dominance and giving more of myself to a man who has done nothing but treat me contemptuously.

He pulls my hair until my head is tipped further.

I feel slight pressure on my scalp, but it isn't painful. Lust shoots through me, exploding like a firework in my core and dampening my panties.

"I'm not sure what to do about you, princess." His teeth sink into my earlobe, sending another arrow of pleasure-pain flying through me.

The hand pressed against my collarbone slides down to my chest. He traces my left breast and draws circles around the perimeter. Every rotation brings his fingers closer to my nipple. More sensation bursts in me when he grazes the stiff peak. With renewed energy, I squirm as he pulls and tweaks the hard bud.

"Don't fucking move a muscle," he commands harshly, dropping his fingers to the middle of my blouse. One by one, he releases the ivory discs from their holes until the material parts to reveal a delicate pink bra.

Roman inhales sharply. His fingers delve into the lacy cup and palm my breast before pushing the fabric down to free it. His gaze meets mine in the mirror. "Do you want my touch?"

God, I wish I didn't.

"Yes," I whisper.

His fingers dive into the other cup, sliding the lace down until air kisses both breasts. "Gorgeous," he growls, playing with one nipple and moving to the other. "So fucking lush."

I moan and wiggle against the erection digging into my back. My tummy trembles as he trails his fingertips down the middle of my ribcage until they hover over the waistband of my skirt.

"Have you let him touch you?"

I purse my lips together. What I've done with Drew is none of Roman's damn business.

His fingers slip under the band and slide straight into my panties. A moan slips free as he cups my naked heat. My body is already dancing on the edge. It won't take much to push me over. The sight of us in the mirror—him holding me with his hand wrapped in my hair, forcing my head back while my breasts spill out of my bra—is the most erotic thing I've ever seen.

I want to burn the image into my brain.

"Have you let him play with your pussy, princess?" He squeezes my slick heat possessively as if claiming something that belongs to him. Roman nips my ear. "Have you?" He squeezes me again and asks, "Do you let him play with this pussy? *My* pussy?"

I blink, thinking I must be dreaming, but the sensual image shimmering in front of me doesn't waver or dissolve.

One thick finger sinks into me. I can't stop the whimper of pleasure from leaving my lips. His grip on my hair tightens, his mouth settling along the curve of my jaw. His bared teeth sink into my skin.

"No," I say on a gasp. Because my physical need for him overwhelms my sensibilities, I wiggle against him seeking more contact.

"Good girl." He pushes in deeper and drags his blunt-tipped finger out. "I'm going to make you come, and when you do, it's my name you're going to be screaming. Do you understand?"

Tears sting my eyes. Roman Santori is a drug pumping through my system. I may not want to be hooked, but I am.

None of my fantasies were ever like this. The sheer dominance he exudes is breathtaking. How does Roman know that it's exactly what I need?

What I secretly long for?

Staring at my reflection in the mirror is like looking at a stranger. A woman with hunger in her eyes gazes back at me, pleasure flickering across her face from the man sinking a finger into her body.

I'm exposed and vulnerable, which is what Roman wants. Yet he gives nothing to me in return. He won't let me breach the barrier he's built around himself.

I blink as reality crashes over me and struggle against his hold.

He chuckles and tightens his grip on my hair to the point of pain.

A frustrated sob leaves my throat. I clench around the thick digit still lodged in my body as it thrusts in and out of me.

"Shhh," he croons. "Doesn't that feel good? Isn't it exactly what you want? What you need?" He continues working me with soft, sure strokes that send arousal swirling through me. "You want this, don't you?"

I don't know why he bothers to ask when he knows damn well that I want him.

The finger inside me glides over my soaked flesh until it reaches my clit. In a matter of seconds, I writhe uncontrollably against his hand.

"That's it, baby," Roman groans. "Come for me." He continues strumming the tiny bundle of nerves until it pulses and throbs. A scream of pleasure builds inside me. "Open those pretty little eyes of yours, Sofia. I want them trained on me when you fall apart."

I do as he commands, knowing I'm about to dive headfirst off the precipice.

His teeth sink into my neck as he pinches my clit. With my hips gyrating, I scream as sensation explodes and ricochets from head to toe. He plunges two fingers deep as my core convulses around them. I babble his name over and over.

His velvety tongue soothes the area he's bitten as he watches me come down from the high. He unseats himself, leaving emptiness in place of the fullness that filled me to the brim. As I watch in stunned silence, Roman brings his fingers to his mouth and sticks them inside. His eyes close for a beat and then reopen, hitting me with raw intensity. "So fucking good." He brings the digits to my lips. "Open."

My lips immediately part, and his fingers slide into my mouth.

"Suck them, princess." His voice sounds gravelly.

I obediently suck, faintly tasting myself on his flesh. My core dampens with renewed excitement. There's something incredibly erotic about this experience.

"When you return to your boyfriend, I want you to remember who made you come and how loud you screamed my name." He releases my hair and pulls his fingers out of my mouth, leaving me bereft. With his eyes locked on mine, he flips the lock on the bathroom door and disappears into the hall.

I gulp a lungful of oxygen as if I'm starving for air. Feeling off-kilter from the encounter, I stumble to the sink and grip the porcelain until my knuckles turn white. I gasp at my reflection in the mirror. I look like I've been fucked.

With trembling hands, I tuck my breasts back into my bra and button my shirt. I run my fingers through my hair, trying to tame the wild-looking mass. As I give myself the once-over, I notice a faint bite mark on my neck.

Need crashes over me like a tidal wave as I lightly run a finger over the indentation. How can I be aroused again when I just came?

I splash cold water on my face, trying to gather my scattered thoughts. It takes another five minutes for me to pull myself together before I return to the bar where Drew waits amidst the chaos of jostling bodies, loud music, and flickering lights. From beneath lowered lashes, I search the immediate vicinity for Roman, but he's nowhere to be found. My nerves twitch as I sense him watching me from somewhere in the club.

"Here's your water." Drew hands me a bottle with a grin.

"Thanks." I twist off the cap and guzzle half the contents, but the cold liquid does nothing to douse the inferno raging inside me.

CHAPTER TEN

"I had a great time tonight." Sincerity swims in Drew's green eyes. "I'm glad we were finally able to do this."

I force a smile. "Me, too. It was fun." Unfortunately, that's exactly the way it feels. *Forced.* I can't imagine getting together with him again. Nor can I imagine this relationship progressing any further. Not when I have such strong feelings for someone else. And not when I allowed one man to touch me when I was out with another.

Oh my God, who does that?

I'm not that kind of person.

I'm not, damn it.

I study Drew's face, desperately wanting to feel a tenth of what I feel for Roman. But I just don't.

Until my run-in with Roman, I'd had a great time with Drew. I'd forgotten about Roman and the intense feelings he rouses in me for a few hours.

I'm embarrassed for responding to him the way I did and humiliated for melting in his arms right after he touched me. I have no willpower when it comes to that man.

I blink, and Drew's handsome features blur in front of me before solidifying.

Drew was a complete gentleman this evening. In the year and a half that we've worked together, he's taken the time to get to know me and expressed interest even though I continually shut him down. I wish his efforts were enough. I wish I felt even a spark of attraction.

By the time we pull up in front of my house, I just want the evening to end. I want to go inside and scrub Roman out of my mind and off my body while taking a hot bath.

What occurred tonight can't happen again. I thought staying away from him would be enough to make me get over him. Clearly, that's not the case. I'm in deeper than I was before.

Drew turns off the truck and angles his body toward mine, blissfully unaware of the fact that another man fingered me in the bathroom and derailed the course of the evening and our entire relationship.

I think he's waiting for an invitation to continue our date inside my place. Up until an hour ago, I'd berated myself for not giving him a chance sooner. I realize now that he'll never stack up to Roman.

"I hope we can do this again soon," Drew says, breaking the silence.

Even though I don't see that happening, I can't convince myself to tell him. "That would be nice," I remark weakly.

His expression flickers with confusion and falls in disappointment. He reaches over and takes hold of my fingers. Unlike the previous times he did this, I feel nothing. The budding feelings of attraction that buzzed through my body earlier are gone.

I feel bad for wasting his time. But instead of explaining that what happened tonight has nothing to do with him, I bite my tongue.

I can barely admit the truth to myself, let alone him.

Feeling like crap for ending the night on such a strange note when it had started out so promising, I say, "It's late. I should probably get inside."

The hopeful glint in his eyes dies out. "Oh. Yeah, sure."

For the first time this evening, awkwardness descends.

I lean toward him and lay a chaste kiss on his cheek. Before Drew can take it further or ask questions, I grab the handle and push the door open.

"Sofia?" Drew calls. "I enjoyed spending time with you and getting to know you better."

Bending at the waist, I meet his gaze. "Me, too."

"Good night."

Relief rushes through me. "Night, Drew. See you Monday." I slam the door and hurry up the cement walkway. Once I reach the front door, I turn and wave.

Drew continues watching me as I rummage through my purse for my house key, which makes me want to smack myself for not giving him more of a chance.

I slide the key into the lock, twist it until there's a click, and turn the handle. Pausing, I wait for a series of high-pitched beeps from the security system my father installed after I purchased the house last spring.

They don't ring out, which is odd.

Drew pulls away from the curb as I lock the door. His red taillights disappear into the darkness.

I know I set the alarm before we left. But when I glance at the panel, it's already been disengaged.

Stepping into the living room, I flick on the light switch. A noise draws my attention to the corner. I freeze, my gaze darting over to the leather armchair.

And the man sitting on it.

CHAPTER ELEVEN

"How did you get in here?" I squeak out.

Instead of answering, he stares at me in an unnerving fashion that makes me feel like I just invaded *his* home. One side of his mouth curls into something that resembles a smile as he stretches his long legs out in front of him.

I knew I set the alarm before leaving earlier with Drew. Roman managed to disengage the system without setting it off and alerting the authorities. My father assured me that I had a state-of-the-art security system. Merely tampering with the locks on the windows or doors trips the alarm. It's happened a few times in the past.

"Your security system is child's play." He absently strokes the dark stubble on his chin. "I'll have to speak with Enzo about that. You need to be upgraded."

The absurdity of his words brings a gurgle of laughter to my lips, and I raise a brow. "Oh? And what will you tell him? That you broke into my house in order to test the system and found it lacking?"

His eyes narrow, and all the humor flitting across his face vanishes.

"Why are you here?" I force out the question, even though I already know the answer.

Images from the club flash through my mind. What we looked like entwined in the mirror above the sink. His hands gliding over my body. His teeth sinking into my neck. My hair wrapped around his fist.

He rises from the brown leather chair and stalks toward me.

Spellbound, I stand rooted in place, caught in the crosshairs of his gaze. The closer he gets, the harder my heart thuds.

When he's no more than a foot away, he grinds to a halt. "What happened between us, it's not enough."

I agree. The fifteen minutes we spent together wasn't nearly enough to satiate my hunger for him. "It shouldn't have happened in the first place," I say in spite of the way I still long for his touch and crave his dominance.

"You're right, it shouldn't have," he states in a frank tone. "But it did. And now I want more."

Stepping closer, he lifts a hand and softly grazes my cheek. "I shouldn't have laid one goddamn finger on you. That was my first mistake." Anger kindles in his eyes as he rasps, "Now the floodgates have been opened, and there's no turning back. I walked away earlier and allowed you to run back to that other guy. What I should have done is taken what I wanted. I should have thrown you over my shoulder, carried you out of the club, and taken you home myself."

Desire rushes through me, warming me from the inside out. It's something only he is capable of stirring to life. I don't understand why, but feel addicted to it nevertheless.

I know I should tell him to leave, but the words stick in my throat as I bask in his gentle touch.

Roman caresses my other cheek. "I'm going to fuck you nice and hard, princess. I'm going to give us what we both want. What we need from each other. And when I bury my cock deep inside your sweet pussy, you're going to scream my name just like you did earlier."

His crass words light a fire under my skin and make me picture us naked and fucking.

In the far recesses of my clouded mind, I know that us having sex will only intensify everything I feel for him.

Or... is it what I need to move on? To dispel the attraction simmering beneath the surface?

He cradles my face in his palms, tipping my head until our eyes meet. "You want this, Sofia. I know you do. We've wanted it for a long time," he says silkily.

I've never heard him sound so cajoling. As if he's trying to entice me onto a path I've never considered. But I have. Many times before. Which only makes it all the more seductive.

I nibble my lower lip, vacillating between what I know is right and wrong. He wants physical release, and I want one night with the man who has haunted me for way too long. I can't bring myself to say no and deny both of us, so I murmur, "Okay."

His lips crash into mine. I open for him right away, and his tongue plunges inside, tangling with mine. He didn't kiss me at the club, so I revel in the feel of it now. I'm greedy for his mouth.

I have no idea what tomorrow will bring, but right now, I don't care. I refuse to dwell on it. I'm going to enjoy this moment.

Tomorrow is soon enough to find myself buried beneath a mountain of regret.

Roman's hands slide down to the top of my blouse. With deft fingers, he flicks open each button and divests me of the shirt. He unsnaps my bra and tosses it to the floor. His gaze falls to my breasts as he palms them.

I moan as he plucks my nipples, my eyes drifting shut as arousal builds in my core.

He flicks the clasp of my skirt and lowers the zipper, pushing the fabric over my hips and down my thighs until it pools around my ankles. His eyes rake over my body, twin flames igniting in them as he takes in my thong, thigh-high stockings, and heels. "Goddamn, you couldn't be more perfect."

I glory in his approval and the reverence in his gaze. I lay my fingers in his warm palm without hesitation when he holds out a hand.

He tows me toward him and wraps his arms around me, burying his nose in my hair. "You need a good fucking, princess."

I groan as desire zips through every nerve ending. "Yes."

"I thought so." He lifts me, sliding his hands down to my ass as he carried me to where my bedroom is located at the back of the house.

My covered center rests against his lower abdomen. Letting go of all my inhibitions, I loop my legs around his waist and shamelessly grind on him.

Roman strides into the bedroom and drops me in the center of the queen-sized bed.

I bounce once and lay with limbs akimbo, shivering with anticipation as he looms over me. Wanting to slip my heels off, I lift a foot.

"Leave them on," he gruffly orders.

Liquid heat gathers at my core. Roman's commanding personality makes me weak in the knees. I want to lie back, spread my legs wide, and give him everything he desires. After fighting long and hard for independence from my family, I shouldn't relinquish it so easily, especially to a controlling man like Roman.

But it's precisely what I want.

What I need.

He grabs the hem of his shirt and yanks it over his head, dropping it on the floor. Roman is all carved muscles that flex and bunch with every movement. A strip of dark hair between his ridged abdominals disappears beneath the waistband of his jeans. His fingers flick the button of his jeans and force the zipper down. The material parts, revealing a chiseled V.

My eyes widen because he's bare underneath.

God, that shouldn't be so sexy.

But it is.

Heat simmers in the pit of my belly at the sight of his long, thick erection pressing against the denim. His fingers linger at the waistband. My eyes flick impatiently to his when he doesn't push it down. A corner of his mouth curls into a smug smile because he knows exactly what kind of physical discomfort he's causing me.

A low growl vibrates at the back of my throat.

Taking matters into my own hands, I roll from my sprawled-out position on the bed. I crawl forward until I'm eye level with his open fly. Sitting on my haunches, my fingers peel the stiff material away from his body to free his cock.

Leaning forward, I lick him from root to tip. He groans as I flick the bulbous head and draw it into my mouth.

Roman's hands sink into my hair, holding me in place as I flatten my tongue and rub the sensitive spot where the head meets the shaft. He thrusts his hips in rhythm to my movements.

A long, low groan of pleasure rumbles up from deep in his chest as I take him deeper. Beads of salty precum hit my tongue and whet my desire for this man.

His shaft swells, his balls drawing up tight against his body. But instead of coming, he pushes me away. The head of his cock pops free as I stare up at him in confusion.

He moves a hand to my face and sweeps his fingers across my lips. One thick digit pushes into my mouth. Eyes trained on his, I suck it.

He watches me through heavy-lidded eyes with a satisfied smile. "Do you have any idea how many times I pictured you on your knees, sucking my cock?"

I moan around his finger, eyeing the erection only inches away.

He removes the digit from my mouth and the hand from my hair. "Turn around."

I scramble to do his bidding.

Once I'm in position, Roman places a hand between my shoulder blades and pushes me down until both cheek and chest are pressed to the mattress and my ass is high in the air. He grips my hips and pulls me to the edge of the bed, where he widens my stance.

I shiver as a finger slips under the elastic band of my thong and traces a path between my cheeks. Goose bumps rise as he continues to caress me.

With a sharp jerk, he tears the delicate fabric away. He palms a cheek in each hand and massages them. "Such a pretty pussy," he muses, pulling and stretching the firm globes.

I arch my back to tempt him into touching me. I'm so turned on. So deeply aroused by the way he's fondling my backside that I'm soaking wet.

A sharp slap to my ass cheek rings throughout the silent room. I gasp as the pain dissipates, leaving petals of pleasure unfurling in its wake.

Roman gently rubs the afflicted area. "Beautiful," he murmurs.

He smacks the other side with the same intensity.

My gasp ends on a groan as he tenderly attends to the smarting flesh.

"Does that make your pussy wet?"

I moan in response.

"Perhaps I should check for myself."

I strain against his hold, impatient for penetration.

His touch is as fleeting and delicate as a butterfly wing as he runs his fingers over the outside of my aching lower lips, rimming, but never slipping inside me. When I try arching closer, his other hand moves to the base of my spine, holding me firmly in place.

I whimper in frustration because I thought he would take me fiercely. But Roman is intent on drawing out the exquisite pleasure-pain he's invoking in me. My nerves tingle, my senses heightened as I wait for how he'll lay his hands on me next.

As much as I love the torture, my body longs for release.

The possessive hold on my back disappears. Once again, he grabs a cheek in each hand and parts them. I moan in ecstasy when his tongue swipes over my slit. Needing more, I push against him.

He chuckles. "Greedy, aren't you, princess?"

Unable to form a coherent thought, I whimper and fist the bedspread as he takes a long, slow lick.

"Delicious." Roman sucks my throbbing clit, driving me higher and higher.

When I can't stand a moment more, when I feel like I'm going to splinter into a million pieces, he presses a kiss against my opening and spears his tongue into my hot sheath. Pleasure floods my system.

"So creamy wet. I want to lick every last drop from your sweet pussy, but I can't wait a moment longer."

Thank God.

I nearly weep with relief. I don't think I can take any more of his teasing.

Before another thought has time to register in my brain, he buries himself to the hilt inside me. The feeling of being filled to the brim is like nothing I've ever experienced. My entire body sighs in contentment.

I explode after the fifth thrust. My inner walls spasm around his girth, and he groans, pounding into me harder before collapsing against my back. The way his body drapes over mine is comforting. It's like we've done this a hundred times before. A sense of rightness settles over me as his heavy breaths mingle with my quick ones. Having Roman inside my body feels like a homecoming of sorts.

Everything in me stills as that thought takes up residence in my brain.

The feelings he's managed to rouse within me are dangerous. I need to push them away, tamp them down, pretend they don't exist. I close my eyes, expecting him to pull out and gather up his clothes—

Wait a minute...

Did he even bother to discard his jeans?

Oh my God!

I become aware of the coarse material pressing against my flank and the zipper biting into my backside.

I giggle because the fact that we've done this is crazy.

"What?" he asks, sounding relaxed and satiated.

"You didn't take off your jeans." As soon as the words escape, I chew my lower lip, realizing it was a mistake to remind him of what we've done. All he needs to do is tug them up and throw on his shirt. Then he'll walk out the door, and whatever this was between us will be over. Roman hasn't even pulled out of my body, and I'm already mourning the loss of him.

This isn't good.

Roman slips out of me and straightens to his full height. "I can remedy that." He kicks off his shoes—which he also never removed— and pulls the gun out of the holster fastened to his belt, placing it on top of my dresser. Keys and his wallet join the firearm. He shoves the jeans down his muscular thighs and steps out of them.

And then Roman Santori is gloriously naked in my bedroom.

I spread my thighs wide in invitation. He may have just fucked me, but I'm hungry for more. I'm not sure if I'll ever get enough of him.

His gaze drops to my pussy, and his shaft hardens. With a smirk, he crawls onto the bed with me.

Apparently, he's hungry for more as well.

CHAPTER TWELVE

I wake in stages as if fighting my way to the surface. Something feels off, but my mind can't figure out what. I stretch my hand out next to me coming away with nothing but air.

Which is the precise moment when everything from last night crashes into my brain with the force of a tsunami.

Roman.

The bathroom at Covet.

Him waiting in my living room.

Both of us needing more.

I don't remember how many times we sated our hunger for one another. He woke me three or four times during the night. It was, in a word, delicious. So much better than any of my fantasies.

My eyelids flutter open.

Before I let the regret for making such a huge mistake swallow me whole, I allow myself a few moments to revel in every amazing moment that occurred between us.

Maybe I'm naïve, but I never imagined sex could be so explosive.

Or hot.

Or dirty.

Exhausted from the long night, I arch my naked body until every muscle has been lengthened and stretched. My hair is a wild, tangled mess spread across the snowy white pillowcase. I pick up a long lock and twirl it around a finger, recalling the way Roman wrapped it around his hand. A stab of desire arrows through me and settles like a heavy stone in my core. It hasn't been but a few hours since he was inside my body and I still want more.

With a deep sigh, I sit up. The sheet falls and pools at my waist.

My gaze meets his, and I gasp, caught off guard by the dark, brooding eyes fixed on mine. My heart skips a beat as arousal floods me. Desire follows quickly on its heels. My core dampens, and I marvel at my visceral reaction to him. Roman has always had a strong effect on me.

But now it's much more intense because I know what he's capable of. I'm tempted to hold out a hand and beckon him to me. I don't want this interlude to end yet.

Already dressed, Roman sits on a chair in the corner of the room with his elbows resting on his knees and his hands clasped in front of him. The passionate man who made me scream his name multiple times last night is gone, replaced by an impassive one who's ready to leave.

In a desperate bid to stop the inevitable, I say, "Come back to bed."

Roman's gaze shifts to my bare breasts and lingers for a beat. He shakes his head and runs a hand over his hair. Looking me straight in the eyes, he says in a clipped tone, "Last night was a mistake. I shouldn't have allowed it to happen,"

Even though I suspected this would happen, his dismissive words still sting. "But it did."

He shrugs. "I knew it was a fucked-up idea when I was doing it."

Fucked-up.

He thinks what happened between us is fucked-up.

I shiver as the cool air in the room swirls around me, realizing how exposed I am. Closing my fingers around the sheet, I yank it up to cover myself.

I'm an idiot for thinking we could hold reality at bay for just a bit longer.

I don't understand why he bothered sticking around this morning.

If he'd snuck out at the crack of dawn, I would have gotten the point just the same.

"Then why did you?" Anguish pounds through me as I force myself to hold his gaze.

He drops his eyes, staring down at his clenched fists. "It doesn't matter. None of it does. What happened last night shouldn't have. My control slipped. That's all."

"That's all," I echo in disbelief.

"You have to know that there can never be anything between us."

I latch on to his words because the reason for his past treatment of me hinges upon this rationale. "Why do you say that?"

He remains stubbornly silent.

My breath wedges in my lungs. More than anything, I need to understand why he acts the way he does.

He lifts his eyes. Emotion he normally hides behind a mask of indifference churns in them.

I sit up a little straighter, feeling as though I'm on the cusp of a significant discovery. I want him to let me in. Just a little. I want to understand what's happening in his head.

"Because that's the way it has to be, princess," he says firmly.

My heart twists painfully under my breast, because the nickname that usually grates on my nerves sounds like an endearment. In the past, he's used it as an insult.

I shake my head and climb from the bed, tightening the sheet. I don't understand his answer. And since he refuses to elaborate, I have no choice but to push him.

Roman averts his eyes as I approach him. A muscle ticks in his jaw. He looks edgy, as if he could spring into action any second.

"Roman," I whisper, "look at me."

I've never known him to be a coward.

When he continues to avoid eye contact, I sink to my knees and raise my hand, cradling his shadowed cheek. "Explain to me why we can't be together." I pause, hoping he'll say something, but he doesn't. "Does this have anything to do with my father?" I press, grasping at straws. "Is he the reason?"

His gaze rises and locks on mine. "It has nothing to do with your father."

Hope dissolves. Papa would've been an easy obstacle to overcome. "Then what is it?" I swallow down the nausea roiling in the pit of my belly as a thought pops into my head and choke out, "Is there someone else?"

In the time Roman has worked for my father, I've never heard anything mentioned about a woman in his life. He could be married with kids for all I know.

"There's no one else," he mutters. "It would be so much easier if that were the case."

My tongue darts out to moisten my dry lips. "Then what? I don't understand."

His dark eyes lose all traces of emotion as he stares at me. Through me. He peels my fingers from his face and drops them. "I'll never be the guy you want me to be. Nor do I have any interest. It's as simple as that."

I wince at the harshness bleeding through his voice.

He tilts his head to the side and snickers. "Did you think this was the start of something beautiful? That we would ride off into the sunset together?"

He shakes his head when I don't reply, an ugly smirk twisting his lips. "Come on, you know better than that," he says in a patronizing tone.

I want to argue but can't think of anything to say.

Is that what I thought?

I don't know.

Maybe it was. Maybe I still clung to a speck of hope that things would be different between us.

"Look, do I need to spell it out for you?" Roman snaps. "There is no you and me, princess. There isn't an *us*. There never was, and there never will be. We spent a few hours screwing. That's all it was." He sneers, his teeth flashing against his olive skin. "I needed a fuck, and you were in the wrong place at the wrong time." He reaches over and strokes the side of my jaw. "Although, I'm not going to lie, the sex was phenomenal. I knew you would be an amazing fuck."

Instinct takes over, and I jerk away. My hand slices through the air, the palm connecting with his stubble-roughened cheek. A loud crack rings through the room. Fury bubbles up, and I shake with anger. "Get out!"

He remains seated, fingering the red mark flaring to life across his cheek.

"Get out now!" I scream again, blinking back tears. I don't want him to see me cry. I've already let the asshole see too much, and he doesn't deserve any more.

Roman rises to his feet, his dark gaze softening. He opens his mouth as if to say something but thinks better of it. His expression hardens, and he nods in acceptance. He strides out of the room without a backward glance.

The tears burning the backs of my eyelids fall right after the front door closes. Feeling raw and angry with myself, I drop the sheet and head to the bathroom. I reach into the shower and turn the handle all the way to hot so I can scrub every trace of last night from my skin.

I want to wash away the memories, too, if possible.

Because I can't continue living this way.

I can't continue lusting after a man who only wants to hurt me.

CHAPTER THIRTEEN

"Hey, stranger," Drew says from around the side of my office door. "I stopped by a few times, but you've been busy."

We haven't spoken since our date on Saturday. After what happened with Roman, I've dreaded running into him again.

I smile brightly, hoping it doesn't look as forced and awkward as it feels. "Hey, yourself. This week has been crazy. I've had back-to-back meetings scheduled with students almost every day." I'm aware that he popped in a handful of times because Sherry, our secretary, let me know with a sly grin and a twinkle in her eyes.

"I haven't had a chance to talk with you since Saturday." He studies me for a moment. "I had a great time. I hope you did, too."

"I did, it was a lot of fun."

And it had been up until my run-in with Roman. Unfortunately, that incident made me realize that I'm not ready to begin a relationship with Drew. Or anyone else, for that matter. It wouldn't be fair to start something when my heart isn't in it.

His smile broadens, relief shining in his green eyes. "Good, I'm glad to hear that. If you're free, I was hoping we could get together this weekend. I have concert tickets for Saturday night."

My heart plummets. I nibble my lip while contemplating how to handle this. "Drew," I say carefully, "there's something I need to talk to you about."

Concern colors his expression as he steps into my office and slides onto the seat opposite me. "I'm not trying to be pushy here, Sofia. But I like you, and I thought we clicked over dinner." He pauses and continues in a lower voice. "It's been a while since I've felt this way."

This is *exactly* why I've been leery about getting romantically involved with a colleague. The last thing I want is to have an uncomfortable working relationship with someone. Drew isn't a man I can brush off and hope I'll never run into again. "I had a great time on Saturday. Dinner was fun and the club..." I gulp as unbidden images of Roman flash through my mind.

Much like ripping off a Band-Aid, I need to let him down as quickly and painlessly as possible. "Look, Drew, you're an amazing guy. And I enjoyed getting to know you better. But, at this point, I think we're better off as friends and colleagues."

His face slackens. "What?"

I fidget under the weight of his confused stare and clear my throat. "When I agreed to go out with you, I thought I was ready to move on, but it turns out I'm not. The last thing I want to do is waste your time or lead you on." Gently, I add, "And that's what I would be doing if we continued to see one another."

He shakes his head and mumbles, "I don't know what to say."

I wince. "Just know that this is my issue, not yours."

"Help me understand what happened here, because dinner was amazing. We were laughing and talking and having a great time. We walked over to Covet and danced for a bit, and I thought, the more I'm with this woman, the more I like her. And then," he shrugs, "your entire demeanor changed. You were distant all of a sudden. Preoccupied. I wasn't sure if I'd done something wrong."

I didn't realize he'd felt my withdrawal so keenly. "I'm so sorry. I wasn't trying to send you mixed signals. I just..." Unsure of what to say, I fall silent.

His sandy brows pinch together as he leans closer and rests his forearms on the edge of the desk. "The guy you're not over, did you see him at Covet?"

Oh, God.

Heat floods my cheeks. "Yeah," I admit quietly. "He was there." It's the truth, just not all of it. Reaching across the desk, I cover his hand with my own. "I never meant to hurt you."

His expression lightens. "Listen, I had a great time. I'm sorry your ex ruined our evening. I wish you would have said something when it happened. We could have gotten out of there and gone somewhere else." He pauses and adds, "I understand what you're going through. I was with my ex-girlfriend for two years. At the time, I'd thought we would get married. But it didn't work out that way. When we broke up, it took a while for me to feel ready to jump into another relationship."

Relief sweeps over me. "Thank you, Drew. I appreciate that."

He smiles. "It's not a problem." He turns his hand over so that his fingers clasp mine. "I won't lie and say that I'm not disappointed. I am. Saturday was a lot of fun, and I was hoping we were on the same page with starting a relationship." He shrugs. "But we're not. And that's fine. I'm a big boy, and I can handle it."

I squeeze his fingers. "I wish things could be different. You're a great guy, Drew, and I enjoyed getting to know you better."

"I can give you more time if you need to sort things out in your head. I haven't met a lot of women I've clicked with right away, but you're one of them."

My brows shoot up. Isn't he aware of the fan club he has here at Lincoln High? There have to be at least six young female teachers who would be thrilled to have his interest.

"What?" he asks, looking adorably confused.

A small smile tugs at the corners of my lips as I shake my head. "I'm just surprised to hear you say that."

"Well, it's true. I'm interested in connecting with someone on an emotional level. I want a solid foundation of friendship and attraction." He shrugs. "I really do like you, Sofia."

"I like you, too," I murmur.

There may not be a spark between us now, but maybe there could be if I work through my feelings for Roman. It seems wrong to not leave the door cracked open.

Drew smiles. "If there comes a time when you're ready to try again, just say the word. It's your move to make."

"Okay. I'll keep that in mind."

Releasing my fingers, he stands. "A couple of us are stopping at O'Toole's after work to grab a beer. You're welcome to join us if you want."

Even though we've agreed to shelve a romantic relationship for the interim, spending time with Drew in a group setting seems like a good way to continue getting to know him. "I wish I could, but I have a tour scheduled at three o'clock. A family interested in moving to the district wants to check out the school."

One side of his mouth curls as his nose crinkles like he just caught a whiff of something rancid. "On a Friday afternoon?"

The last remnants of tension dissolve as I laugh at his disgusted look. "Yeah, I know, but they're from out of state, and this was the only time they had available. It probably won't take more than an hour—"

"Well, if you're up to it, swing by O'Toole's afterward. I'm sure we'll be there for a while."

I turn the offer over in my head. "Maybe I will."

His smile grows wider, revealing a row of straight white teeth.

I almost shake my head while marveling at how he's taken my rejection in stride. Not many men would. My thoughts veer from the seemingly perfect man in front of me to the one who rejected me with the same shitty excuse of "you were in the wrong place at the wrong time."

I'd be a fool to let Drew walk away while continuing to pine for a man who isn't worth my time.

As he crosses the threshold of my office, I blurt, "I'll try to stop by after the meeting."

He flashes me another bright smile. "Great. Hopefully, I'll see you around four or so."

I nod, proud of myself for taking this much-needed step. Our first date didn't go exactly as planned, but there's no reason why we can't get back on track.

Roman is my past.

With some emotional purging on my end, Drew could be my future.

CHAPTER FOURTEEN

Hearing footsteps in the outer office, I rise from behind my desk and stick my head out the door. "Mr. Dmitriyev?"

A man with icy blue eyes studies me with an intensity that sends a shiver racing down my spine. "Yes, I'm Victor Dmitriyev." He holds out a hand. "And you're Ms. Bianchi?

I force a friendly smile and step forward. "Sofia Bianchi. Please, call me Sofia." I give him a firm shake. "I'm one of the counselors here at Lincoln High School. I'm delighted you were able to squeeze in a tour before heading home tomorrow."

His gaze leisurely travels around the office, which is empty since everyone already left for the day. "Thank you for sticking around to meet with me. We've been house hunting for most of the day, so this was the only time that worked."

His voice has a slight accent that I can't place. It might be Slavic.

"It's no problem at all. Choosing a school district is an important decision. I hope I'll be able to answer any questions you might have." I fight the urge to fidget as he continues to stare at me. Something about him makes me feel uncomfortable.

"I have no doubt that I will come away completely satisfied at the end of our meeting, Ms. Bianchi." His thin lips curve into a smile that doesn't reach his eyes. It reminds me of Roman and my father's men, which is really odd.

I shake off my paranoia, chalking it up to being out of whack after getting kicked to the curb by Roman. "I thought you mentioned that your wife and son would also be accompanying us for the tour. Are we waiting for them to join us?"

"Yes, well, that was the original plan. But we were all up early this morning. My wife and son are tired after looking at houses all day. They decided to stay back at the hotel. I know what qualities my son is looking for in a school, so that won't be a problem."

I nod since his excuse for their absence is plausible. "All right then, I suppose we should get started."

Since it's just the two of us, I hope this can be wrapped up in about thirty minutes. Drew's invitation sits in the back of my mind. The more I think about it, the more I want to stop by O'Toole's for a drink. We had such a great time at dinner, and I want to see if it's possible to recapture that feeling.

"Excellent," Mr. Dmitriyev says, gesturing for me to lead the way with an extended arm.

We start out on the main level, where the media center, main office, cafeteria, music and art hallway, computer lab, and student lounge are located. I have keys for all the rooms, so we pop in and look around at each one. Along the way, we run into the principal. Like me, Mr. Atherby is working late. The two men shake hands after my introductions. Mr. Atherby makes small talk for a few minutes and excuses himself.

I've given more than a dozen tours of the school during my two years here, so I have my spiel down pat. As we walk through the halls, peeking inside classrooms, I explain which AP classes are offered and where our district and high school rank in the state. I mention the athletic teams and clubs that round out our academic experience.

I show Mr. Dmitriyev the gym and pool, pointing out the athletic fields. The weird vibe I felt earlier still vibrates beneath the surface, but I push it aside to deliver all the pertinent information he and his family will need to make a well-informed decision.

"Does the school offer any auto mechanic classes?" he asks.

"As a matter of fact, we do. All of the technology labs are on the lower level. Would you like to check them out?"

"Yes, I'd like that. Alex is very interested in working with his hands." He offers me another cool smile that makes him look like a shark. "Just like his old man."

I shiver and try to brush off my discomfort while plastering on a courteous smile. "Of course. Follow me."

We head to the closest stairwell that leads to the basement. Without any natural light filtering in, the hallway is gloomy. Art students painted vibrant murals across the long stretch of concrete walls to brighten up the area. The fluorescent lights on the ceiling are activated by a motion sensor and flicker on as we reach the bottom step.

The auto mech lab sits midway between the two stairwells. I point out the other technology classes we also offer—welding, CNC, and machine shop—as we walk down the corridor. Since his son seems interested in cars, I fill Mr. Dmitriyev in on the credentials of our teaching staff. I also tell him about the agreement the district has with one of the local technical schools that enables students to continue their education after they've exhausted our course listings at no cost to the parent.

Victor doesn't say much. He seems to be quietly absorbing everything. I tend to throw a lot of information at parents because there are so many great things happening at Lincoln High and in the surrounding community.

As we arrive at the double doors for the auto mech area, I slide the key into the lock. I don't want to rush through the last part of the tour, but there's something I don't like about this man.

As I turn the handle, he roughly grabs me from behind and rests something on my throat. His other arm snakes around my waist and hauls me against his hard body.

Shock and panic grip me. "What-what are you doing?"

Victor's warm breath drifts across my ear. "You need to listen very carefully, Sofia, and do exactly as I say." He presses the cold metal further into my jugular until it breaks skin and continues in a low, sinister voice. "You won't enjoy the consequences if you don't, and I'd hate to see blood spilled all over your pretty shirt."

A knife.

He's holding a knife to my neck.

My mind empties. All I can focus on is the warm blood trickling down my throat.

"Do you understand what I'm saying?"

I'm afraid to deepen the cut by breathing or swallowing or nodding. Tears fill my eyes as he presses down harder. "Yes," I whisper.

"Good girl. No one needs to get hurt." He chuckles. "At least not yet, they don't."

"What do you want?"

The heaviness of the blade stays firmly pressed against me. If I try to move, it'll slice right through my jugular. The way he holds both me and the knife suggests this man is a professional. Too late, I realize I should have listened to the warning bells ringing in my head instead of dismissing them as paranoia.

"There's a message that needs to be passed along to your father."

"My father?" I ask, confused about why he matters right now.

"Yes, Enzo Valentini." Again, he chuckles. "Did you think we weren't aware of the connection? That we weren't keeping tabs on you? That we couldn't take you anytime we wanted?" His paper-dry lips press against the side of my face. The smell of cigarette smoke tinges my nostrils, making me nauseous. "Were you foolish enough to think that you could change your name and no one would realize who you were? That you couldn't be dragged back into your father's world if we had need of you?" He makes a soft clicking sound of admonishment with his tongue.

"Sorry, sweetheart, it doesn't work that way. Although, you certainly made it easy. No security or guards. Out in the open, ready for the taking. All I had to do was make an appointment, and you came right to me."

Spikes of fear careen through my body because everything he said is true. I'm used to moving anonymously through my life. It never crossed my mind that someone would come to the school and hurt me.

Closing my eyes, I try to calm my racing thoughts by taking deep, even breaths. "What do you want me to tell my father?"

"All in due time." He loosens his hold on my waist and snakes a hand up my body to cup my breast. "I'd heard you were a real stunner. Now we get to meet in person. Lucky us."

I try shifting out of his grasp, and he presses the knife harder. Stilling my movements, I whimper in pain.

"Ah, ah, ah. I wouldn't wiggle around too much if I were you." He squeezes my breast, digging his fingertips into the soft flesh.

"Please, don't," I plead.

He kisses the side of my face. "If another chat becomes necessary, I'll do far more than mark up your neck." Again, his fingers bite into me. "Got it?"

"Yes."

"Good. Nothing pisses me off more than having to repeat myself."

Victor drags his tongue across my cheek. "You tell Enzo that the next time he steals a shipment from us, his beautiful daughter is going to disappear. But don't worry, you'll be returned one piece at a time." He snickers. "Of course, we could always take a road trip to Philadelphia. Wouldn't it be fun to surprise your sister with a visit?" He laughs at his own joke and continues. "Neither of you are safe. If Enzo values his family, he'll return what he stole from us. Understand?"

"Yes," I whisper hoarsely, repulsed by the way he licked me and terrified by his threats. Squeezing my eyes shut, I pray for him to leave now that he's delivered his message. I cry out when his teeth sink into my earlobe.

"Good. I told them that with two college degrees, you were one smart cookie. Maybe we'll run into one another again, hmm? You have such a charming little house. Although that alarm system isn't so good. Very easy to circumvent." He exhales a harsh, nicotine-tinged breath. "You're a restless sleeper. Did you know that? Many nights I've watched you toss and turn." He presses his face against my neck. "I know what could help with that."

My knees weaken at the thought of this bastard breaking into my house, hovering over me, and watching me sleep. I have no idea if he's telling the truth or trying to scare me.

"There's nowhere you can hide that I can't get to you." To emphasize his words, he viciously pinches my breast. His hand and the knife disappear.

Unable to move, I keep my eyes tightly screwed shut while struggling to accept that this ordeal—this *attack*—is over. Bile rises up in my throat as the staccato clicks of his wingtips striking the tile floor grow fainter.

Shock takes over, and my knees give out. I crumble to the floor in a heap.

My fingers tremble as I gingerly touch the cut on my neck. Pulling my hand away, I look down at it. There isn't as much blood as I'd imagined. As I sit on the floor, I realize that nothing but silence surrounds me. On shaky legs, I force myself to stand and bolt toward the stairwell at the other end of the hall, in the opposite direction from which we came. I can't chance running into Victor Dmitriyev again.

Although I'm willing to bet he's long gone.

He did what he came here for.

Now he'll wait for me to deliver his message.

CHAPTER FIFTEEN

"Until the situation has been resolved, you'll move back to the compound immediately." Papa adds, "And you'll also take a leave of absence from your job."

"You can't be serious!" I shake my head. "I'm not moving to the compound. And I won't quit my job!"

Papa leans across his desk, rage filling every line of his face. A muscle ticks near the corner of his eye. He's holding onto his temper by a thread.

I understand that his fury is fueled by fear. He's livid that someone dared to lay hands on me and threatened his family. But still, I can't be expected to stop living my life.

"Sofia," his voice cracks like thunder in the silence of the office, "I will *not* allow anything else to happen to you. Do you understand me?"

It's on the tip of my tongue to point out that whatever he took from the Russians is precisely why I was ambushed and threatened. But I don't. I refuse to lash out at him for wanting to keep me safe.

Attempting to wrangle my heightened emotions, I suck in a deep breath and slowly blow it out. Then I try again. "Papa, I'm not leaving my home. Nor will I take time off from work. I love my job too much to jeopardize losing it."

What I've accomplished in my career has nothing to do with the Valentini name. And I'm proud of that. I secured my position as a counselor because of my hard work and dedication. I won't allow my father's business dealings to take it away from me.

"There are other jobs, Sofia. We'll find you another, I promise. This family has plenty of connections all over the city. All over the goddamn country, for that matter. I'll buy you a damn school if that's what it takes."

"What? No! I don't want that!" I exclaim. "You can't just buy a school. It doesn't work that way." Yelling isn't going to get us anywhere, so I soften my tone to keep the argument from escalating. "Papa, please. I love this job, and I don't want to step away from it. There has to be another way, something else we can do until the situation is handled."

He bangs his fist on his desk. "Why do you have to be so stubborn?" Huffing in frustration, he throws his hands in the air. "You're just like your mother!"

A smile trembles around the corners of my lips in spite of the seriousness of this situation. Whenever I would dig in and refused to cave during my childhood, my father would throw his hands up and tell me I was stubborn like my mother.

Maybe I am.

Just like Mama, I know how to stand my ground and fight for what matters most to me. He's not taking away the life I've painstakingly built for myself.

"You'll need security," he says begrudgingly.

"I don't want security," I counter, internally railing at the idea of someone trailing after me and lurking outside my house at night. I cherish my independence and anonymity and wish I'd done a better job of being inconspicuous.

"I know you enjoy your freedom," Papa cajoles, placing a hand over his heart. "But you have to understand where I'm coming from. There's no way I can leave you to your own devices, left unprotected and vulnerable to the animals that have already come after you." He opens his arms wide, hints of fear swirling in his dark eyes.

The urge to keep fighting fades as I realize my father is genuinely frightened for me. I don't want him or my mother to worry needlessly, so I sigh and meet him in the middle. "Fine. One guard. That's it." My eyes narrow. "But I don't want security while I'm at school. I can't have one of your men shadowing me inside the building." I shudder at the thought.

Every bit of Papa's controlled anger breaks free. "But that's where you were attacked!" he shouts.

"I know." I learned my lesson the hard way. "I placed myself in a weak position by meeting with someone after most of the staff had left the building. I should have had one of the principals accompany us. And I should have insisted the tour take place during school hours. It won't happen again, I promise."

My father strokes his clean-shaven chin, seemingly pacified by my words. "I would never forgive myself if something happened to you, Sofia," he says, his voice filled with uncharacteristic emotion.

"I know, Papa." It tears me up inside that he blames himself for this. "I swear, I'll be more careful from now on. I thought I'd taken enough precautions by using Mama's name and a house alarm. I grew complacent in my own security, and I shouldn't have."

His shoulders slump. "We all have. And that needs to change."

What happened is an ugly reminder of what my family is involved in and the reasons I chose to distance myself from it. It's also a reminder that no matter how much I've tried to remove myself from it, I can be dragged back in on a whim. I now realize that the life I created for myself is nothing more than an illusion. I'll never be free of the past or the choices my family has made.

Papa stabs a button on the intercom system and barks, "I want to see you in my office."

Less than sixty seconds later, a discreet knock hits the door. Whoever has been summoned doesn't wait for my father to give permission to enter.

Roman's nearly black eyes lock on mine as he strides into the room. His gaze dips to my neck, and his jaw clenches. He turns to Papa and asks, "What happened?"

Most men would wait for Enzo Valentini to speak first.

But not Roman.

"Those Russian scumbags. They've assumed that we're the ones responsible for their missing shipment of goods." Fury once again fills Papa's voice as he waves a hand in disgust. "As if I have any interest in the product they're moving."

Roman's steely expression never falters. "You want me to set up a meeting? Have a conversation?"

A gurgle of laughter falls from my lips. Whatever happens with the Russians will have little to do with conversing. My father has tried to become more legitimate over the years regarding his endeavors, but that doesn't mean he's gone completely soft. Whoever's involved in what happened today will pay dearly. No one messes with Enzo Valentini's family and lives to tell the tale. The man who held that knife to my throat will die a painful death.

A knot forms in my gut. I don't want blood on my hands. But I know better than to interfere. My father won't listen to anything I say when it involves people who have actively targeted his family.

Papa shakes his head. "Let's figure out what happened first. *We'll* find who stole the shipment before we make any moves. We need to find out who Victor Dmitriyev works for."

Roman frowns. "Dmitriyev?"

My father nods.

"Sounds familiar. Maybe he's with the Vikashev crew?"

"Marco will run the name. For now, Sofia needs protection." Papa jabs a finger in Roman's direction. "And I want *you* to handle it."

What? Oh, hell no!

I assumed Roman was called into the office to take care of—which is a nice way of saying *eliminate*—the problem, not be my babysitter. After what happened last weekend, I don't want to be anywhere near him. I want to forget that he even exists, which I can't do if he shadows me. "Papa," I begin.

My father cuts me off by holding up a hand. He levels me with a glare and bellows, "There will be no more discussions! Roman will protect you until the threat has been eliminated. And that's final!"

"But—"

Raising his brows, he bites out, "Or you move back home and quit your job." He sits back in his chair to await an answer.

Well, hell. He's not leaving me a choice.

I scowl at Roman, who hasn't glanced at me once during this conversation.

Roman clears his throat. "May I speak with Sofia privately?"

My father would automatically refuse if anyone else asked, but he trusts Roman implicitly. That being said, Papa would probably strangle the younger man with his bare hands if he knew we'd had a one-night stand.

I'm tempted to tell him, but I won't.

The only person I blame for sleeping with Roman is me. I knew it was a mistake, and I did it anyway.

My father stands. He's tall and broad-shouldered and prides himself on wearing impeccably tailored suits. For a man over sixty, he's aged well. When I look at old, dog-eared pictures of Papa, he looks a lot like my brother, Matteo. But then again, everyone in my family bears a striking resemblance to each other. We all have thick dark hair, wide espresso-colored eyes, and olive complexions.

"Good luck trying to talk sense into that one. She's always been stubborn." He sighs and heads for the door, pausing at the threshold to glance back at me. "Just like her mama."

I roll my eyes.

He wouldn't have my mother any other way, and we all know it. Papa loves and respects Mama with every fiber of his being.

The door closes with a soft click, leaving Roman and me alone in the office. I have no idea why he asked to speak privately with me. As far as I'm concerned, we have nothing to discuss. Everything that needed to be said came out Sunday morning before I slapped him and screamed at him to get out of my house.

Refusing to look at him, I sit ramrod straight, facing forward with my hands folded neatly in my lap. He's the one who asked to speak with me, so if he has something to say, he'd better get to it. It doesn't take long for the silence to turn suffocating. I break down and reluctantly glance in his direction.

Our gazes collide, and my heart flutters. One look is all it takes to make my pulse kick.

I grit my teeth, loathing the attraction that continues to hum through my veins. It needs to go the hell away.

Roman crosses his arms over his chest. "Look, I know you don't want me around."

That's an understatement. Pressing my lips together, I avert my eyes and ignore him.

"Your father has given me an order, and I'm going to fulfill it." He doesn't move from the wall he's leaning against. "I'll do my best to stay out of your way. I'll give you as much distance as I can." He pauses and then continues after a few beats of silence. "You won't even know I'm there."

Unable to hold my amusement in, I snort. Loudly.

I'm still hyperaware of him. The way I reacted when he walked through the door proves his cruel words didn't kill my feelings for him.

I would dearly love to throw his offer of protection in his face, but I can't. I've already pushed my father far enough. He wasn't kidding about me moving home or quitting my job. If I request a different guard, he'll get suspicious and question me, which I don't want.

Rising from my chair, I take a fortifying breath and turn to face Roman. "I don't have a choice in the matter, now do I?"

He doesn't flinch at the sarcasm in my tone or shift his eyes from my glare.

It feels like we're playing a silent game of chicken, and I refuse to be the loser. Not again.

Roman pushes off the wall and closes the distance between us. He stops close enough for the woodsy scent of his aftershave to fill my nose. His eyes focus on my throat. Rage flickers across his face, vanishing just as quickly as it appeared.

I blink, wondering if I imagined it.

He reaches out and gently grazes the shallow cut.

My breath catches in the back of my throat. Even after the ugly things he said Sunday morning, my body continues to long for his. I order myself to stay still as I squeeze my eyes shut.

"Look at me, Sofia," he demands roughly.

My eyes automatically open and meet his, taking in the steely resolve shining in them.

"I'm not going to let anyone hurt you again. For the time being, you're stuck with me. Where you go, I go."

I shake my head. *No, no, no!*

"Yes."

"Tell him you won't do it," I whisper pleadingly.

His fingers settle under my chin. "No."

"Why?"

"Because Enzo trusts me to keep you safe."

I don't know how I'll survive his forced proximity. This could go on for days, weeks, or God forbid, months.

Even though I know it's useless, I try one last time. "Please don't do this."

He shakes his head. "It's already done, princess."

CHAPTER SIXTEEN

Roman enters the house first, disarming the new, improved alarm system and silently checking every room to make sure they're clear.

I think his precautionary measures are ridiculous. The image of someone hiding in a closet or under the bed while waiting for an opportunity to ambush me is so absurd that I have to suppress a snort.

It's been a week since the incident at school, and there haven't been any other attacks. I have no idea what's going on with the Russians other than the issue hasn't been resolved, which means there's still the potential for retaliation. Quite frankly, I'm not interested in the nitty-gritty details.

I just want my life back.

I can't pretend it's business as usual with Roman shadowing my every move. There's never a time when I'm not aware of him, which is frustrating in and of itself.

Roman meets me at the school each afternoon. He parks a few rows over from my car and follows me home. He enters the house with me, checks every nook and cranny to make sure everything's fine, and heads back to his car to sit for the rest of the night. As promised, he stays out of my way as much as possible.

Every so often, I peek out the window and see him sitting in the darkness, watching the street. If any of my neighbors think it's suspicious that a strange man is parked outside my house, no one's commented on it. Which is for the best, because I don't know what I'd tell them. I keep trying to concoct a story in my head, but none of them sound plausible.

I've had the same nightmare every night since the incident. Almost as if it's playing on a loop in my subconscious, I dream of Victor Dmitriyev hovering over me with a knife in hand, whispering that he's glad there was a next time.

I wake covered in a thin film of sweat, a hoarse scream trapped in my lungs and my heart thumping wildly. It takes a moment for me to calm down. I creep to the living room window and draw back the curtain to make sure Roman is still there. Seeing him awake and alert in his car always settles my frayed nerves. With a sense of reassurance, I climb back into bed and fall into a restless sleep.

At half past six in the morning, he knocks on the front door to make sure everything is as it should be before following me to work in his nondescript sedan. Once I'm safely inside the building, Roman goes home to sleep. He returns at three in the afternoon, and the routine starts all over again.

My father suggested another guard sit in the school parking lot during the day, but I nixed that idea. Roman, surprisingly, backed me up. Lincoln High has its own security guards at the front entrance, and all other exits are locked and set with alarms. I'm surrounded by people throughout the day, so I'm safe. I don't leave the building unless I decide to grab lunch off-campus.

After the fifth night, I took pity on Roman and told him he would be more comfortable sleeping in the guest bedroom. He initially chafed at the offer but eventually caved. Instead of a nightmare waking me up that first night, I barely slept knowing he was twenty feet down the hall from me.

The last two nights have been better.

Uneventful.

The nightmares have abated.

I hope the situation with the Russians will be resolved soon, so both of us can get back to our lives and away from each other. I'm not sure how much longer I can go on with Roman underfoot.

CHAPTER SEVENTEEN

As we leave the school parking lot the following Thursday, I text Roman to let him know that I need to stop at the market and pick up a few ingredients for dinner.

I usually don't cook during the week, but there's something enjoyable about preparing a meal that will be eaten with another person instead of scarfing down a bowl of cereal at the kitchen counter or in front of the TV.

Roman silently walks beside me in the store as I pick up chicken breasts, a wedge of fresh parmigiana, noodles, and sauce since I don't have time to make my own. My mother would keel over if she found out I'm eating, let alone serving, jarred sauce.

The way Roman stands next to me while I pull boxes and cans from the shelves feels ridiculously domestic, like we're an ordinary couple shopping for groceries. Once I realize what I'm doing, I shove the fantasy aside. Imagining a romantic relationship between us is laughable. Intellectually, I understand this. But my heart isn't ready to accept the inevitable. All this forced proximity isn't helping matters either.

Once we get to my house, I dredge the pounded chicken cutlets in egg and then a flour mixture seasoned with Italian herbs and grated parmigiana. I pan-fry the meat, cover it with sauce and mozzarella, and stick it in the oven. Mama used to make chicken parmigiana once a week when we were growing up because it was a family favorite.

Now that I'm on my own, I rarely make it because it's too much work for one person.

When the chicken is baked and the noodles are boiled, I call Roman to the kitchen, and we sit down to eat. Again, my mother would have a coronary if she knew I was serving boxed noodles at my dinner table. She makes all her pasta fresh from scratch. I often came home from school and found racks of drying pasta all over the kitchen.

The meal itself is a quiet affair. Roman says nothing if I don't make an effort to pull conversation from him. He just shovels food into his mouth, which—I'm not going to lie—is satisfying after the effort I made. Oddly enough, the silence hanging over us isn't uncomfortable.

But there's only so much I can take. Halfway through the meal, I blurt, "What's your problem with me?"

It's almost comical the way Roman's fork stalls in midair. His gaze locks on mine from across the table as he sets the utensil on his plate. "What makes you think I have a problem?" he asks, shifting uncomfortably in his seat.

My brows skyrocket toward my hairline.

Is that a serious question?

I almost laugh at the absurdity of it.

"In the three years we've known each other, you've never said one kind word to me. In fact, it's been the exact opposite."

He glares, a hunted expression flashing across his face.

If Roman thinks he can intimidate me into dropping or changing the subject, he's sadly mistaken. His behavior has bothered me from day one. And I deserve an answer.

"Just be honest," I say. "You're not going to hurt my feelings any more than you already have. I'm immune to your personality." That last part is a lie, but this is my opportunity to finally get an explanation, and I'm taking it.

A muscle ticks in his jaw. "You shouldn't be consorting with your father's men."

That's not an answer, and we both know it.

"I don't think exchanging simple pleasantries can necessarily be called *consorting*," I scoff.

He picks up his water and guzzles half the glass.

He's stalling.

Forgetting about the unfinished chicken on my plate, I push it aside and rest my elbows on the table, leaning toward him. "What did I ever do to piss you off? Right from the start, you had a problem with me."

Roman's jaw clenches again as he looks everywhere but at me. "You didn't do anything," he mutters. "It was never like that."

I shake my head, more confused than ever. Does he have a reason for hating me or is he just a jackass? I'm favoring the jackass theory right now. "Then what was it like? Explain it to me," I demand angrily, "because I've seen you be nice to my mother as well as my sister. You're fine with my brothers. And even Grace."

The hunted look is back in full force. It's the weirdest thing. I'm not sure what to make of it.

He sighs and scrubs a hand over his face. "It's my issue. It doesn't have anything to do with you, okay?"

Nothing to do with me?

"No," I snap. "It's not okay. There must be *something* about me that rubs you the wrong way. You've never given me a chance to prove that your initial impression was wrong."

I know he doesn't want to discuss this topic. But I'm done with walking on eggshells and avoiding him. And I refuse to feel like I've done something wrong. We're going to clear the air right here and now.

Roman folds his arms across his chest, his biceps popping with the movement. "I'm not getting into this with you," he says testily. "It's just better for both of us if I keep my distance. I work for your father. There's nothing more to our relationship than that." He pushes away from the table and stands. "I'll be outside. Lock the door behind me."

Disappointment swirls through me. As ordered, I lock the door and pick up the plates, dumping our unfinished meal into the garbage.

Not only have we both lost our appetites, but I'm no closer to understanding his behavior than I was before.

CHAPTER EIGHTEEN

My eyelids snap open as a shrill, earsplitting sound fills the air.

The house alarm has been triggered, I realize.

Roman bursts through my bedroom door wearing only a pair of unbuttoned jeans and clutching a gun. He grabs me by the elbow with his free hand and hauls me out of bed.

He freezes when the sheet slides off of my body to reveal I'm not wearing pajamas, his fingers continuing to bite into my flesh. When I wince, he comes alive and drags me to the bathroom.

"Stay in here until I return," he orders gruffly.

"What's going on? Did someone break into the house?" My mind conjures up an image of Victor Dmitriyev, knife in hand, coming for me just like he promised. A sliver of fear scampers down my spine.

"I don't know, but I'm sure as fuck going to find out. Don't open the door for anyone." His gaze turns stern. "You got it?"

I nod and move further into the bathroom. Even though his eyes never deviate from mine, I'm uncomfortably aware of my nudity.

"And find something to cover yourself up with," he snaps, slamming the door in my face.

I went to bed in a tank top and underwear up until tonight. But I was restless and uncomfortable. Once Roman began staying in the guest room, I decided to sleep as I normally did—in the buff.

I'd considered calling my father to ask him to call off his guard dog after Roman stalked away from the dinner table because everything had been quiet for almost two weeks.

As far as I was concerned, Roman's presence in my house—in my *life*—was unnecessary.

Thank goodness, I hadn't done that. Or I would be here alone, facing whoever's out there by myself.

Locking the bathroom door, I snatch my robe off the hook and wrap it around my body. It's short and silky and doesn't leave much to the imagination. But then again, it wasn't designed to.

I sit on the closed toilet seat and fold my arms across my chest. Every little noise sends me into a full-fledged panic. Roman is the best there is, but I still expect Victor—or another man like him—to come crashing through the door. I shudder while recalling how he held the knife against my throat, the way he squeezed my breast, and how he licked the side of my face.

I jump off the toilet seat when the door handle rattles. My eyes dart to the small window, and I wonder if I can squeeze through it if necessary.

Doubtful.

There's nowhere for me to go. I'm trapped.

"Open the door, Sofia," Roman says.

Exhaling in relief, I lunge for the door and turn the handle with shaky fingers. Our eyes meet for a moment, but then mine drop to his bare chest. And then lower to the unfastened fly of his jeans, where I follow the trail of dark hair until it disappears under the denim. Roman clears his throat, and my eyes snap back to his.

"I didn't find any signs that the windows or doors had been tampered with. I'm not sure what happened." He shrugs. "Maybe it was a false alarm."

I study his closed-off expression. "But you don't think so?"

"No."

"Why not?"

He arches an eyebrow. "Has your alarm ever gone off for no apparent reason?"

Point taken.

"No," I admit.

This is a new alarm. It could be sensitive. But since nothing has been settled with Victor Dmitriyev, I doubt this is a coincidence. The most likely explanation is that the Russians' impatience with the missing shipment is showing.

"I'll take a closer look at the security footage in the morning and see if anything pops up. If someone was out there, they're long gone by now. I checked the neighboring yards. They'll be expecting reinforcements to show up. Nothing more is going to happen tonight."

"Okay." I tighten my robe around myself. "I guess it's safe to go back to bed then."

Roman doesn't move from the doorway, so I slip past him, my body brushing against his half-naked one. Desire slides through me and pools at my core. Even though I'd been scared out of my mind moments ago, my body still responds to him.

"You might want to consider sleeping in pajamas from now on," he grates out.

I glance over my shoulder. My mouth dries when our eyes lock, and I see the hunger in his gaze. I may have told myself that I was moving on, but I haven't. For reasons I don't understand, this is the man I want.

I nod. "Okay."

Roman takes a cautious step toward me. "Do you always sleep in the nude?"

I shrug. "I like the feel of the sheets against my skin." Ever since I bought my own house, I've foregone any clothing at night. It feels... freeing. And it's my house, so I can do whatever I want.

He curses under his breath and shoves the gun into his waistband. Then he gives me a slow once-over.

The air between us electrifies as we stare at each other.

Not giving any thought to the repercussions, I release the edges of the fabric and allow the robe to part. The luxurious material clings to the tips of my breasts, giving Roman a full view of my body.

His jaw locks, the tightly held muscles ticking under his skin as his eyes drop to the valley between my breasts, the smooth skin of my belly, and then my thighs. His gaze lingers on the V between my legs, sending another wave of desire cascading over me.

Drawn to him, I close the distance between us.

He backs away toward the door leading to the hallway, eyeing me warily. "What are you doing?" he rasps.

I have no idea.

But it feels *amazing*.

His typical cold detachment is gone. Roman looks anything but indifferent. The way he watches me with rapt interest makes me want to push his buttons.

I take a deep breath and shrug out of the robe, letting the material puddle around my feet.

Roman's dark eyes widen, the pupils dilating, and roam over my body. "Sofia..." he chokes out.

Standing naked in front of him feels freeing. Like I'm finally taking control of the situation. If he won't give me the answers I seek, I'll push until I figure them out for myself.

"I'm going to bed," I say casually, fighting off the urge to smile. "It's late, and I have to be up early for work in the morning."

"Aren't you going to put something on?" he asks, his voice sounding raw.

For the first time, I feel like I've managed to wrestle control away from him. I *love* it.

Meeting his gaze, I shrug. "Why should I?"

His teeth snap together at my blasé answer.

"You said nothing more would happen tonight." Throwing his own words back at him makes me feel giddy and light. "If anyone was out there, they're long gone, right?" I blink innocently. "But if you're concerned, you could always join me in here."

Fire burns in his eyes.

The proverbial devil sitting on my shoulder spurs me to add, "Think about how much safer I would be with you next to me in bed."

"No!" Roman roars, his face beet red. He looks like he's about to explode.

Which is… interesting.

And oh-so-very satisfying.

He glowers at me, his hands fisted at his sides.

I turn toward the bed, giving him a view of my naked backside. "All right then. Good night."

Still, he doesn't budge.

Excitement dances in the pit of my belly. And lower. *Much lower.* Unable to stop myself, I toss a sultry look over my shoulder…

And catch him staring at my ass.

He looks torn.

"Sure you don't want to join me?" I ask huskily.

His startled gaze snaps to mine. He scowls and storms out of the room, slamming the door behind him.

I wince as the door rattles on its hinges and release a pent-up breath.

He stomps down the short hallway and bangs his bedroom door shut as well.

I've never seen Roman fly off the handle. Not like this. His restraint is one of the qualities that make him such an asset to my father and the organization. He's unflappable.

But his control slipped tonight, which is confirmation that I really do affect him.

Maybe I shouldn't have pushed him to his breaking point, but I'm glad I did. He doesn't want to give me answers, and that's fine.

I'll get them a different way.

CHAPTER NINETEEN

When the alarm goes off the next morning, I throw off the covers and get dressed.

The aroma of coffee hits me full force as I leave my bedroom. I head to the kitchen, stumbling to a halt when I find Roman sitting at the table with a steaming cup in his hands.

I thought for sure he'd make himself scarce and avoid me like the plague after my brazen behavior last night.

My cheeks heat as snippets flash through my mind. I'm still not sorry for pushing his buttons.

His reaction had been worth it.

I take a fortifying breath to steady my nerves and smile at him. "Morning."

He continues to stare at his mug, grunting something unintelligible that could either be "good morning" or "fuck you." Apparently, Roman Santori isn't a morning person.

Shrugging off his surliness, I grab a mug from the top shelf in the cupboard and pour myself a cup. I add a small scoop of sugar along with a dash of cream, then take my first sip.

It scalds as it slides down my throat.

Which is precisely the way I prefer it.

I toast a slice of wheat bread, slather it with butter, and slip into the seat across from Roman.

He warily watches me over the rim of his mug, angling his body toward the door. He looks ready to bolt at any second.

I smile, pleased with myself for shaking him to the core with my impromptu striptease. Part of me hopes he's afraid that I'll tear my clothes off right now.

His glare intensifies, as does the suspicion filling his eyes.

I'm tempted to tell him what I find so amusing, but I doubt he'd find it as humorous.

I should be embarrassed about what I did last night. I've never done anything like that in my life. I've never wanted to. But then again, there's never been a man I wanted as much as I want this particular one.

What surprised me most was the way Roman ran from my bedroom like his damn ass was on fire. Almost like he was *frightened* of me.

That ridiculous thought makes me want to laugh hysterically.

Roman Santori scared of me.

Yeah, right.

"What's so damn funny?" he grumbles, eyeing me cautiously.

I do my best to contain my mirth. "Nothing."

A flicker of annoyance crosses his normally impassive features. "Seems like something."

"Nope, nothing at all." Nothing I'm going to share with him, anyway.

Grunting again, he continues drinking his coffee. "You're awfully chipper this morning."

As I open my mouth to speak again, I realize that *he's* engaging *me* in conversation. Well, this is certainly a first.

Marveling at the flip in our usual dynamic, I say nonchalantly, "All things considered, I slept pretty well last night." I fell asleep right away and didn't wake until the alarm clock went off.

Since there were no further incidents like he assumed, I expect him to say the same. After a few beats of silence, I ask, "You didn't?"

His eyes narrow. "No. I slept like shit."

"Oh?" Again, I'm surprised by the strange give-and-take of our conversation. "How come?"

Still glaring, he bites out, "Just did."

"Hmmm. That's weird. I've always thought the bed in the guest room was comfortable. You don't find it so?"

"The bed is fine."

"Good. It has to be better than catching a few hours here and there in your car."

Sounding downright ornery, he mumbles, "Maybe I should consider doing that from now on."

I shrug as if I don't care either way. I'll never admit it, but I sleep better knowing he's down the hall. The nightmares have stopped, and that has everything to do with Roman staying in the house with me. Rising from the table with my plate and mug in hand, I set them both in the sink and turn to face him. "Suit yourself."

As our gazes lock across the tiny kitchen, a spark of desire zips down my spine. Simply being in the same room with Roman sends need hurtling to the surface.

Breaking eye contact, his eyes fall to my breasts. The frown lines bracketing his mouth deepen. "Is that what you're wearing to work?"

I glance down at my cream-colored blouse, black pencil skirt, and heels. Teachers are allowed to dress casually in khakis and polos, but counselors and administrators are expected to wear business attire. My work wardrobe is filled with skirts, sweaters, blouses, and wool pants.

"Yes." I frown back at him. "Why? What's wrong with my outfit?"

I've worn this ensemble a dozen times throughout the year. No one has ever commented that it's inappropriate. While we're encouraged to dress professionally, I make a concerted effort to appear approachable to the students. Wearing a suit to school doesn't necessarily convey that message.

His expression darkens, storm clouds gathering in his eyes. "Don't you think it's a bit revealing?"

My mouth falls open.

Revealing?

This?

With more scrutiny, I glance down at myself. "What are you talking about? I'm not showing any cleavage." I've caught several teenage boys staring when they thought I wasn't paying attention. Unfortunately for them, I have excellent peripheral vision. "And my skirt hits mid-calf." Irritated that Roman's making me second-guess my fashion choices, I cross my arms over my chest and wait for him to elaborate.

He waves a hand at the general vicinity of my chest. "Your top is a bit snug. I'm just saying you might want to change."

I gasp.

How dare he!

My blouse is *not* snug! It's formfitting. I have large breasts, and I look heavier than I am if I wear loose shirts.

Gritting my teeth, I stomp over to the refrigerator and grab my lunch from inside. "Go to hell."

The table has once again been turned.

Not bothering to say goodbye, I leave Roman sitting alone in the kitchen. I snatch up my briefcase and purse in the entryway and grab my keys from the ceramic bowl near the front door, catching a glimpse of myself in the beveled mirror hanging above the credenza. Stepping in front of it, I examine my reflection with a critical eye, giving extra scrutiny to my breasts.

I have no idea what Roman is talking about.

The blouse is neither snug nor revealing.

He woke up on the wrong side of the bed this morning and is taking his bad mood out on me. I'm not sure if his attitude stems from the possible break-in that woke him in the middle of the night or...

Me dropping my robe in front of him.

Why would that bother him? It's not like he hasn't seen me naked before. We spent the entire night together in bed doing unmentionable things.

I shake my head at the questions chasing each other around my brain.

Why do I care if Roman's upset?

Why am I dwelling on it?

Why am I dwelling on him?

Like everything else involving Roman Santori, I have no answers. He's an enigma I'll never understand. I shouldn't waste any more time trying. And I shouldn't let him get under my skin like an annoying rash.

I shoulder my bags and slam through the front door to head to my car.

Roman comes through the door and locks it behind him as I crank the engine. He looks at me while heading to his sedan.

Because I'm still irked by his comments, I flip him the bird.

Instead of his face turning thunderous, the edges of his lips tip up as he chuckles.

His reaction makes me angrier. Throwing the car into reverse, I peel out of the driveway. I don't have to look in the rearview mirror to know that Roman is a car length behind me. I feel his presence.

Neither of us wants this connection, but it still hums between us, more powerful than ever.

CHAPTER TWENTY

As usual, the final bell rings, and students flood out of the school before I can catch my breath. Most of the teachers are right behind them. I've been booked solid from the moment I stepped into my office with student appointments, two parent meetings, and class scheduling for next year.

I normally leave at three, but I stayed after for twenty minutes to finish up paperwork for an early meeting on Monday morning. As I walk down the hall toward the back doors leading to the teacher parking lot, I hear someone calling my name.

Recognizing the voice, I turn and wait for him to catch up. "Hi, Drew."

"Hey! How's everything going?" He grins.

"It's good. Busy as always. How about you? I heard you took your physics class to an amusement park on Wednesday. Everyone have fun?"

His smile widens, white teeth flashing in that easy, relaxed manner of his. He tosses his head, his dark blond hair moving from in front of his green eyes. "Are you kidding? Of course, they did. I'm beginning to suspect that most of my students take physics so they get a free trip at the end of the year. Maybe you can tag along as a chaperone next time." He teasingly elbows me in the side. "You know, see physics in action."

I laugh. "Maybe." It could be fun.

Bright sunshine warms our faces as we push through the heavy glass doors. May has brought gorgeous weather with its arrival. The students, along with a good number of the staff, are already climbing the walls, in the throes of spring fever. We've caught more than a few students trying to sneak out of the building to cut classes. It's difficult to blame them when the weather is this beautiful, especially after the long winter we endured. But still, everyone needs to keep it together for a couple more weeks, and then we'll all be able to enjoy a well-deserved break.

Drew nods toward a group of teachers standing in a huddle, talking in the parking lot. "A few of us are heading to O'Toole's to grab a beer and throw darts. I thought since your meeting ran long last time, you might be up for joining us."

My smile falters as Victor Dmitriyev's face flickers through my mind. Fear suffuses me as I recall how the knife felt against my neck and how he manhandled me while whispering threats in my ear.

Drew knows nothing of the attack because I didn't tell him about it. I haven't discussed it with anyone other than family.

I couldn't report it to the administration or police because it would take less than thirty minutes for the local authorities to figure out I'm a Valentini. And then the life I worked so hard to create would be ruined. I refuse to allow someone with a vendetta against my father to take away my freedom.

Inhaling deeply, I push all the ugly memories to the back of my mind, where I lock them away and plaster a smile on my face.

Drinks with coworkers seem like a nice way to end the week. Maybe I should take Drew up on his offer.

Just as I'm about to tell him that a beer and darts sounds like fun, the fine hairs on the back of my neck rise. Glancing around the half-empty lot, I glimpse Roman watching us from a few rows away. His eyes are covered with dark sunglasses, but the heat of his gaze singes my skin. Hot, molten lust rushes through me and pools in my core.

I force my eyes back to Drew. "I would love to," I say gently, "but I can't."

He steps closer and asks in a low voice, "Just out of curiosity, does this have anything to do with the guy parked in the car over there?"

My eyes widen. "*What?*"

Drew jerks his head in the direction of Roman's nondescript sedan. "He's been watching us the entire time we've been talking." He arches a brow at me. "Or, I should say, he's been watching *you*. I noticed him as soon as we walked out of the building."

My mouth dries as I scramble to come up with an answer. "Yes," I admit, "it has everything to do with him."

Eyes turning hard, he straightens to his full height. "Is this guy giving you problems? Stalking you or something? Do you need help?"

My lips tremble at the corners as I shake my head. "No! I don't need help. It's not like that at all."

The look he gives me is full of doubt.

"Drew," I try again, "you have it all wrong. He's not stalking me. I promise. In fact, your assumption couldn't be *further* from the truth."

He glares suspiciously in Roman's direction. "Then why is he here?"

I clear my throat knowing that while I can skirt around some of the truth with Drew, the details regarding why Roman's waiting for me isn't something I can discuss. That would only open up a can of worms I'm unwilling to deal with. "I asked him to meet me."

He cocks his head to the side. "Would you tell me if you were in a bad situation?" Reaching out, he grabs my hand and squeezes it. "Look, I'll help you any way I can. Just say the word, Sofia."

Forgetting that Roman's watching us like a hawk ten yards away, I lift my hand and cradle the side of Drew's clean-shaven face. I glimpse the longing in his eyes as they soften. I wish I could give him what he wants. And I wish I wanted it as well. My life would be so much less complicated if I could fall for a man like Drew.

"We're not together." Sucking in a breath, I force it out gradually and tell the truth. "Our relationship has *never* been like that. He," I pause, searching for the right words to explain our situation, "works for my father. I'm interested, he's not."

Drew bursts out laughing, and my hand falls away in surprise. "Oh, come on! How can you say something so ridiculous? Any man would be lucky to have you. You're gorgeous, sexy, and smart."

Heat stings my cheeks at the compliment. "Thank you for saying that, but—"

He squeezes my fingers. "No buts. It's the truth. All I can say is that if he's not into you, then there's something wrong with him. You're perfect in every way."

I choke back the argument poised on my tongue and accept his kind words. "Thank you."

"Well, I'd hoped that you'd be ready to give us a try in a couple of weeks or months, but by the look on your face, that doesn't seem very likely. I think it's going to take more time than either one of us thought before you're over that guy."

My teeth sink into my lower lip because I suspect his assessment of the situation is probably correct. "I'm sorry about this."

He smiles ruefully. "You have to love the irony of the situation. You're hung up on some guy, and I'm hung up on you." He shrugs. "I don't know, maybe it's time for both of us to consider moving on."

A chuckle escapes as I shake my head because it's the best advice I've received in a long time. "You might be right about that."

"Well, there's nothing I can do about my situation, but there is something I can do about yours," he says, his eyes sparkling with mischief.

Before I have a chance to ask what he's talking about, Drew tugs on my hand, reeling me closer. He wraps his arms around my waist and draws me in until my breasts flatten against his chest.

His face is so close that his breath feathers across my lips. "You ready for this?"

A grin pulls at the corners of his mouth as it descends onto mine. The kiss lasts for ten seconds. Maybe fifteen. By the time I process the fact that Drew is kissing me—that this is actually happening—he's already pulling away.

He winks. "FYI—I've wanted to do that for a really long time."

My brows shoot up as I gape in shock.

He slides his fingers under my chin and gently closes my mouth. "That good, huh? I rendered you completely speechless?" His smile broadens. "Trust me, the pleasure was all mine, and I'd be willing to do it again."

His playful manner makes me burst into giggles. I can't believe he did that! And in the school parking lot, no less! I glance around furtively, relieved that no one is paying us any attention. Gossip about a kiss like that would spread like wildfire. Everyone would know about it by the time I walked into school Monday morning. I should be mad at Drew for taking such liberties, but I'm not. I think he was just trying to help.

Drew's eyes shift to the side. "If the scowl is any indication, your friend doesn't look pleased. Maybe he's not as indifferent as you think he is."

My eyes dart in Roman's direction. With the aviators covering his eyes, I can't tell what he's thinking. Drew's right, though—Roman appears to be glowering. But there's nothing unusual about that.

"That's his normal expression," I mutter.

"Interesting. So, you're into the dark and brooding types, huh?" He scratches his chin. "I'll have to work on that."

Turning back to him, I say, "Don't you dare! I like you just the way you are."

He smiles. "Good to know."

"Thank you," I say, grateful for how he set aside his own feelings to help me with another man.

"Like I said, it was my pleasure entirely." He lets go of my hand and steps away. "Well, I should probably get going. Those darts aren't going to throw themselves. Plus, I have the feeling that if I keep you detained any longer, that guy is going to come over here and pound the hell out of me, and I don't think my ego could take that."

"Okay."

He gives me a wave. "I'll see you on Monday. Have a great weekend." His expression turns earnest. "Just remember, if you need anything—anything at all—you can always give me a call. Got it?"

"I will," I promise, although I know that won't be necessary. "Have a good weekend, too."

I sneak another peek at Roman while heading to my car. His features look as though they've been carved from stone. I grew up with men who keep their emotions firmly in check, never allowing anyone to glimpse too much. I get it. It's a necessity in their line of work. But Roman has one of the best poker faces I've ever seen.

The drive to my house takes less than fifteen minutes, which barely gives me enough time to clear my head before I have to face him. His sedan stays a car length behind me the entire time. If I change lanes, he swiftly follows suit. It's comforting and nerve-racking at the same time.

A knot forms in the bottom of my belly after I pull into my driveway. Roman enters the house first to make sure the place is clear. I wait a couple of minutes and go inside.

The front door is ajar. Stepping across the threshold, I pause, listening for Roman's whereabouts. I don't know what to expect from him after the last twenty-four hours. I'm not sure where we stand with each other.

As I move further into the foyer, I glance toward the living room and find him parked on a leather chair with his elbows resting on his knees. He rolls his shoulders while staring at me, and I mentally prepare myself for whatever is about to happen. The air is charged with explosive energy. Roman has the ability to shrink a space that should feel open and airy into something oppressive.

"I thought you were done with him," he says.

Ignoring his question, I ask one of my own. "Why does it matter? I'm free to see whomever I want."

He's out of the chair and stalking toward me in the blink of an eye. I scrabble backward as he closes the distance between us. The air rushes out of my lungs as my back hits the wall.

Looming over me, he snarls, "You're playing a dangerous game, princess."

"I'm not the one playing games," I retort with renewed strength. "I've been very clear about what I want, Roman. It's you who continues to send mixed messages."

Boxing me in with his body, he places his forearms against the wall on either side of my head. "Don't you understand that I'm trying to do what's best for both of us?" he asks in a voice that sounds rough as sandpaper.

"I never asked you to."

His heated gaze drops to my lips.

For an agonizing moment, I wait for him to lean in and kiss me, but he doesn't. Instead, a growl rumbles up from deep in his chest.

He jerks away, taking his scorching body heat with him. Looking frustrated, he plows a hand through his short hair and walks toward the front door.

"You're leaving?" Disbelief echoes throughout my words.

With his back to me, Roman's broad shoulders slump as he pauses. "Yeah." His back straightens as he grabs the handle.

This is what he does, I realize with a flash of insight.

The morning after we slept together.

Last night.

Now.

He's running away from me.

I swallow down my disappointment and ask in a steady voice, "Where are you going?"

Opening the door, he throws a glance over his shoulder, his mask of cold indifference back in place. "Nowhere that concerns you."

His response feels like a slap to my face. There's something about his agitated demeanor that suggests he's leaving for good. Panic surges inside me at the thought of not seeing him again. Even though I'm tempted to go after him, I force myself to stand still.

I can't keep chasing Roman.

Blinking back tears, I ask, "Are you coming back?"

"I don't have much choice, now do I?" he snaps bitterly, slamming the door behind him.

I flip the lock and set the alarm, tracking Roman as he passes the other plain sedan parked at the curb.

Roman nods at Marco and slips into the driver's seat of his own vehicle. He must feel the weight of my stare because he glances over at me after starting the engine.

Our gazes lock and hold briefly.

He breaks contact first and drives away, leaving me to pull myself together again.

CHAPTER TWENTY-ONE

Unable to get comfortable, I huff in frustration and roll onto my side. I've slept soundly ever since Roman moved into my house, easily falling into slumber and waking well-rested in the morning.

But not tonight.

His absence has me unable to relax or shut off my brain.

Unsure if he would show up, I prepared dinner and ate alone in silence. Then I spent the rest of the evening flipping through two counseling manuals I ordered online and peeking out the window to see if Marco was still sitting outside the house.

He was. Instead of packing up the leftovers, I put together a plate and brought it out to him. At first, he was taken aback by the gesture but quickly accepted my offering.

I decided to turn in around ten. I'm still wide awake at eleven when the front door opens and closes. The hallway floorboards creak under Roman's footfalls. My breath catches when he pauses outside my closed bedroom door. I'm tempted to get up and open it, but don't. If anything is ever going to happen between us, Roman has to make the first move. *He's* the one struggling with his feelings. *He's* the one who refuses to give in.

Instead of knocking, he continues toward the guest room at the end of the hall, softly closing the door behind him.

Disappointment floods through every fiber of my being as I turn over. Lying on my side, I squeeze my eyes shut and pray for sleep to take me now that Roman has returned.

Another two hours of restlessness creep by, and I'm no closer to falling asleep than I was before. Feeling agitated, I throw off the covers, deciding a hot cup of tea might help settle my nerves. I grab my robe from the hook in the bathroom. This time, I tie the sash securely around my waist to hold the material in place.

The house is silent as I pad into the kitchen. I flip on the small light above the sink and yelp in fright when I turn to find Roman sitting at the table.

His dark, brooding gaze is already locked on mine.

My hand flies to my pounding heart. "Roman! You scared the hell out of me! What are you doing sitting here in the dark?"

My gaze drops from his face to his bare chest, where it lingers with appreciation on his ripped, sinewy muscles and perfectly formed pecs. His flat brown nipples harden under my unabashed scrutiny. Gulping, I ball my hands into fists to stop myself from reaching out and stroking my fingers over all that tightly harnessed strength.

His brows lower as he takes in my flimsy robe. His gaze burns across my body, awakening every nerve ending. Desire scuttles through me, settling in my core and pulsing with need.

"Couldn't sleep." He looks just as churlish as he did this morning. And then later this afternoon when he stormed out.

I want to ask him what that was about, but I keep the question to myself. I don't want to push him any further away than I already have.

A tall glass of water sits on the table before him. His hands rest on his thighs as he continues holding my stare.

"Me, neither." Needing something to occupy my hands, I turn toward the cupboard, reaching for a mug and a box of decaf tea. I would normally set a kettle on the stove to boil, but it's late. Instead, I fill a cup with water and put it in the microwave, setting the timer for sixty seconds.

Even though I try to avoid looking at him, his body is like a magnet, and my gaze finds its way back to him. "You were gone for a while," I say, leaning against the counter.

Breaking eye contact, he stares down at his glass. "There was business that needed to be taken care of."

"Is it over?" My body tenses. "Has the situation with the Russians been resolved?" The thought of all this craziness coming to an end and getting some much-needed distance from Roman should thrill me.

Oddly enough, it doesn't.

"No. Not yet. It's become something of a delicate situation."

Relief sweeps through me. I don't want him to leave. Not yet. Not before whatever this is between us has a chance to get resolved.

He sucks in a breath and gradually releases it as if the weight of the world rests on his broad shoulders. There's a weariness about him that bothers me. It makes me want to go to him and smooth out the furrowed lines on his forehead.

"I'm tired of fighting this, Sofia. I've tried doing the right thing." He runs both hands over his head. "God knows I have, but I'm done. I can't do it anymore."

My heart stalls as I stare wide-eyed at him. I want to pinch myself to make sure I heard him correctly. That this isn't a dream I'll wake from in disappointment.

"Three years. That's how long I've been fighting this."

Hope tinged with caution wells up inside me. "I never asked you to stay away," I say, my voice low and scratchy.

His stormy eyes meet mine. "I'm no good for you. I'm the last man you should get involved with. You shouldn't even look in my direction."

The truth spills from my lips in a rush before I can rein it in. "I haven't been able to stop looking since I first saw you. This entire time, it's been you."

Frustration pours off him in thick, heavy waves as he drags a hand over his face. "This shouldn't be happening," he mutters to himself. "But I don't have the strength to fight it any longer. I can't keep walking away from you."

The silence is shattered by a series of beeps signaling that the water has been heated, but I don't bother with it. I'd come to the kitchen thinking I wanted a cup of tea, but what I need more than anything is the man sitting at my kitchen table.

I need him like air to breathe.

No longer able to bear the separation, I close the distance until he has to crane his neck to hold my gaze. His eyes turn pleading. I've never seen this kind of raw vulnerability shine from them. Roman shifts uncomfortably under the weight of my gaze, and it makes me fall even harder for him. I want to wrap my arms around him and never let go.

"If you're smart," he growls, "you'll tell me to get the fuck out of your house and never come back again." When I say nothing, he snaps, "Say the damn words, Sofia! Tell me to leave!"

A gurgle of laughter escapes from my lips.

Does he actually think that's going to happen?

Doesn't he understand that I'm powerless to send him away?

I reach out and stroke my hands through his closely cut hair. Electricity zips through me from the contact. "I can't do that." I won't do it. Nothing he says or does could make me walk away from him.

He has to know that he's asking for the impossible.

His gaze pierces mine, full of turmoil and the responsibility and desire that are continuously at war. "I can't give you what you're looking for or what you deserve. A few weeks. That's it," he rasps. "You need to understand that and accept it before this goes any further."

I swallow the argument perched on the tip of my tongue. If Roman needs to set an expiration date on this relationship in order to give in to the desire we both feel, then so be it. I've spent the better part of three years wanting this man, unable to look at or think about anyone else. Whatever his terms are, I'll accept them.

For the time being.

"Who said I wanted or needed anything more?" I lie.

His expression flattens. The look he gives me speaks to all the secret desires I've spun in my head. It's as if he knows every single one of them intimately.

A myriad of conflicting emotions churn in his eyes—anger, lust, fear, remorse, and finally, acceptance.

"Don't you understand that you deserve more than what I'm capable of giving you?" he asks with a hint of desperation.

My fingers trail from his head to his face until I'm able to cradle his bristly cheeks in my palms. "I want you. I always have. Are you going to deny me that?"

It all boils down to that one question.

Will he deny me what I want most of all?

Him.

Eyes searching mine, he shakes his head. "No. I won't deny either of us any longer. For better or worse, this is happening. There's no going back."

With those ominous words, he buries his face in the hollow between my breasts and inhales. The movement warms my flesh and sends shivers careening down my spine. His fingers drop to the belt holding the robe in place around my waist. He unties the knot. The ends of the sash slip free as the silky edges of the material part to reveal my naked body. His hands go to my breasts, squeezing and cupping, palming their heavy weight. I close my eyes, enjoying the sensation of his strong hands on me.

The first time we had sex, that's exactly what it felt like.

Sex.

Fucking.

A simple exchange of pleasure to sate the deep hunger within us.

This feels like so much more.

Exactly what, I have no idea, but I'm going to enjoy it for as long as it lasts.

"You're so beautiful." Reverence is woven throughout his thick voice.

Gently holding a breast in each hand, he uses his calloused thumbs to strum my nipples until they stiffen. He brings his mouth to one and flicks his tongue over the turgid bud. Reveling in the feel of his mouth on me, I pull him closer.

Shifting to the other, he nips at the dusky peak and sucks it deep into his mouth. A whimper escapes as pleasure unfurls deep inside me. His hands move from my breasts to my collarbone, shoving at the material until it slips down my arms and pools at my feet, leaving me completely naked.

Roman comes to his feet. One hand slides around the back of my head and guides my mouth to his. His lips devour mine, hungrily roving over them as if famished. I open, eager for his tongue to mate and dance with my own.

The hand holding my head trails down my back, caressing the curve of my hip and descending further. His fingers spread over the rounded curve of my ass and pull me flush against his body. I feel the heavy ridge of his erection pressing through his boxer briefs.

Another current of electricity sizzles through me. I'm mindless with the need to undulate against the thickness jutting out so prominently. Instead, I dip my hand inside his boxers and grip the hot length.

Roman growls. His fingers bite into the soft flesh of my bottom as he backs me into the counter. With his mouth fused to mine, he picks me up and sets me on the granite. His lips trail along the side of my jaw. My head lolls to the side as he sucks and licks his way down my neck. He caresses every inch of skin, lavishing attention on my breasts and belly until reaching the apex between my thighs.

Breathless with anticipation, I wait for him to dive in. But he surprises me by pulling back, his eyes settling on my throbbing core.

I've never felt more exposed in my life.

And yet...

The intense perusal doesn't embarrass me. I would give this man anything he asked for. I would give him all of myself.

Roman slowly pushes my legs apart until I'm spread wide. My breath comes out in short gasps as he continues to look his fill. I squirm as need lances through me.

Leaning forward, he feathers his mouth over my pussy.

I moan and arch my back, inching closer.

"I've spent years wanting to spread you wide and play with you." His gaze holds mine for a heartbeat and drops back to my center.

I widen my stance, opening myself up more to give him exactly what he wants.

"You have the most beautiful pussy." Roman presses his lips against my aching lower ones. "So pink and lush." He nibbles my delicate flesh. "Soft." He nips my clit. "Delicate." His tongue artfully dances over me and delves into my warmth. "Delicious." With careful fingers, he exposes me even more. Flicking his tongue over my opening, he points the tip and thrusts it inside. "So fucking creamy."

His thumb settles on the pulsing bundle of nerves as he works me with his tongue. Sensation swirls through me, building in my core as he drags his digit over me again and again.

"Warm and welcoming," he mutters, his tongue rhythmically dipping in and out of me.

Needing more, I grind against his hot mouth. My body is strung impossibly tight as I hover on the brink of shattering into a million broken pieces at his hands and talented tongue.

"Come for me, princess," he whispers, applying more pressure to my clit.

I fly over the precipice, repeatedly screaming his name as the strongest orgasm I've ever experienced streaks through every nerve ending.

Roman continues his ministrations with long, slow licks. "There's nothing more beautiful than hearing you scream my name."

When the last waves of pleasure recede, I slump on the counter, drained and thoroughly satisfied.

CHAPTER TWENTY-TWO

I wake with a jolt, my eyes flying open as memories of what happened last night flood my brain.

Jackknifing up, I glance at the other side of the bed.

It's empty.

For a confused moment, I sift through my memories, trying to decide if it was nothing more than an erotic dream or if Roman and I actually ended up in bed together.

An ache between my thighs flares to life as I shift against the sheets.

Definitely not a dream.

I exhale, disappointed yet unsurprised that Roman is no longer warming my bed.

Roman lost the battle against his attraction to me last night. His absence this morning indicates he's still struggling with the idea of *us*.

Flopping back against the pillows, I rehash everything that occurred. How he took me in the kitchen (note to self: scrub counter with anti-bacterial cleanser), then carried me to the bedroom where we made love and fell asleep in each other's arms.

I have no idea when Roman got out of bed or where he went, but he couldn't have gone far. He wouldn't leave me unprotected. He may be angry with himself for caving, but he would never put my life in danger.

Laying there, I rack my brain, but can't figure out his rationale for not wanting to get involved. He's been adamant about keeping me at arm's length until now. He's denied that my father factors into his decision. He also said he's not involved with another woman.

And I believe him.

What other explanation could there be for his reluctance to move forward? No matter how many times I turn the question over in my brain, I can't come up with an answer that makes sense.

I have a better sense of who Roman is after spending the last couple of weeks with him. The armor he cloaks himself with is showing tiny cracks and dents. He's not as unaffected as he wants me to believe.

The unrelenting attraction I feel for him is inexplicable. I've tried severing our connection too many times to count, but the invisible thread binding us has only grown stronger.

I'm startled out of my thoughts by the rattling of pipes as the shower in the bathroom begins to run.

Throwing off the sheet and comforter, I pad toward the bathroom attached to the master bedroom. I tentatively push open the door, my eyes honing in on the man standing under the heavy spray of water in the glass-enclosed shower. The mirror over the marble-topped vanity is already fogging from the steam rising up from the hot water.

Since his back is turned to me, I lean against the doorway and watch as he pours shampoo into his palm. His biceps bulge and flex as he massages it into his hair. My mouth salivates as he ducks under the water. My gaze runs over his muscular back, narrow waist, and firm ass. The urge to run my tongue over and sink my teeth into his taut globes pounds through me. Moving on from his backside, I find well-defined thighs dusted with dark, crinkly hair.

Observing him is enough to dampen my panties.

If I were wearing any panties, that is.

The ache between my legs flares back to life.

His head snaps around, his hot gaze meeting mine as I open the door and step inside. The same kind of hunger that gnaws at my insides darkens his eyes. I slip my arms around him, loving the feel of his naked backside against my belly and breasts. My fingers glide over his ridged abdominals and descend to his erection. I wrap one hand around his thick girth and massage his balls with the other.

He tormented me with his touch last night. I want to return the favor this morning by making him crave me with the mindless intensity that has plagued me for years.

Using my teeth, I nip at his shoulder and leisurely stroke his cock.

He emits an animalistic growl. "If you're looking to get fucked, princess, just keep that up. I'll have you pressed against the wall of this shower in a matter of seconds."

My core bursts into flames in response to his threat. I squeeze his balls, and he groans, his head tipping back until I'm able to stand on tiptoe and press a kiss to the corner of his mouth.

"That feels so damn good."

I capture his upper lip with my teeth, tugging at it. Sparks of arousal flash in his eyes.

With my body brushing against his, I slide around until my breasts press against his chest and his cock digs into the soft flesh of my belly. He watches me through narrowed eyes full of interest as I sink to my knees.

Roman has a beautiful cock. It's long and thick and feels like steel sheathed in velvet.

I lean forward and kiss the slit, tasting saltiness where beaded moisture has gathered. I keep my gaze fastened to Roman's as his fingers thread through my wet hair.

I lick from the base of his shaft to the top of his mushroom-shaped head and settle my lips over the crown. I suck him down as far as possible and slide back to the tip, where I flatten my tongue over the most sensitive bit of flesh, rubbing continuously.

Roman groans. His hips flex as his fingers sink into my scalp, holding me firmly in place.

There's something incredibly erotic about the way we stare at each other as I suck him into the warm haven of my mouth.

All of the muscles in his body tighten. He clenches his teeth, a muscle twitching in his jaw. Another groan rumbles up from his chest.

I focus my attention on giving him pleasure with the same determination he gave me last night. I want his release. I want to shred the last vestiges of his control. I want him to fall apart at my hands.

"Oh God, baby, that feels amazing. Your mouth," he says hoarsely, "is like fucking nirvana."

I feel the same way about his cock. I love the idea of giving him pleasure with not only my pussy but my mouth as well.

My hands slide around to cup his ass. I squeeze the toned flesh and drag him closer.

He releases my hair and tries to pull me up. "I need your pussy, princess."

I want that as well.

But…

I want this more.

"No." I suck him back into my mouth and shift a hand to the front to play with his balls, rolling them between my fingers until they tighten and draw up against his body.

He mutters an oath, the tendons in his neck stretching as his head kicks back.

I focus on him, noting every nuance of pleasure as it crosses his face. Hot water continues to cascade over us.

His body stiffens, and then Roman orgasms, shouting my name like a benediction. His brows draw together as his hips buck into me.

I swallow his warm seed as it streams into my mouth, sucking until there's nothing left and he's softened.

Releasing his cock, I kiss the soft tip and nuzzle the silken head. I don't think I've ever enjoyed giving a man a blow job more.

"Fuck, baby." Roman hauls me off my knees and into his arms.

I smile as he takes fierce possession of my mouth, thrusting his tongue deep, and presses me against the shower wall as the two of us meld into one.

CHAPTER TWENTY-THREE

Roman and I lay entwined on the couch in my living room watching TV. Some sort of action movie is on. I have no idea what the name of it is. Or if there's a plot. Every so often, there's an explosion, gunfire, and a car chase.

Having Roman stretched out beneath me is pure bliss.

I could stay like this forever.

That dangerous thought continues to rattle around in my brain. As much as I push it aside, it stubbornly returns to the forefront of my mind and grows stronger with each passing day.

Once the movie ends, Roman shifts under me. I'm so comfortable that I don't want to budge. I want to find a way to stop time. Or at least slow it down. This is the most content I've ever felt in my life. The thought of this inner peace disappearing as quickly as it came about is painful. I don't think I could bear for our relationship to go back to the way it was. Not after being so intimate with him. And not after opening up and giving him every little piece of myself.

I keep hoping that he'll change his mind about our temporary arrangement. But I have no idea if that's even a possibility. He refuses to say a word about *us*.

I don't know what the future will bring, and it's driving me insane.

I agreed to accept whatever he was willing to give, but it's a bigger challenge than I anticipated.

"Ready for bed?" he asks, skimming a palm from my knee to my hip.

What a ridiculous question.

I'm always ready for bed as far as this man is concerned. No matter how many times we make love, it's never enough. I'm insatiable. I realize that it's partly because what I've found with Roman feels precarious and could end at any moment.

I untangle my limbs from his as that thought spins around my head. Before I can stop myself, I blurt, "Why does this have to end?"

That question is like an explosion rocking both our worlds.

His eyes cloud over.

I've tried so hard not to bring it up. I've tried to let this be a meaningless fling and not push for answers, but it's not in my nature to go along with something I don't understand.

Separating himself from me, he sits on the edge of the cushion and runs a hand over his head. "It's complicated, Sofia." He glances at me with an irritated expression. "Can't you just leave it at that?"

I want to laugh at the absurdity of his request. Now that he's within reach, I can't bring myself to think about the possibility of losing him.

He hasn't admitted that he has feelings for me, but he shows me in a hundred different ways.

I feel them in the reverent way he touches me and the tender way he makes love to me. And I see them in his eyes whenever our gazes meet.

The fact that he'd rather walk away instead of fighting for a future together makes me angry.

"No, I can't. Why won't you tell me what's going on?" I reach over and snag his fingers with my own. "Whatever the issue is, we can find a solution."

Jerking away, he jumps to his feet and paces back and forth like a caged animal.

"Roman," I plead, "tell me what's going on." I've asked this question before, but can't help circling back to it. "Is it my family? Are you afraid they won't approve?"

He couldn't be more wrong on that front. My father loves him as if he were his own flesh and blood. I've never seen him take an interest in anyone who isn't part of our family the way he has with Roman. You'd think my brothers would be jealous of their relationship, but they're not. They're relieved that Papa has found someone strong and capable to assist him. Like me, they each have their own ideas about what they want to do with their lives. And Roman makes it easier for them.

Fed up with the silent treatment, I say, "They would, you know. My father considers you family."

A man like Roman should understand exactly what those words mean. How significant they are.

But he continues to pace as though he hasn't heard a word I've said.

When he reaches the far end of the room, he swings sharply toward me. He plants his feet and stares at me through bleak eyes. "It's not your family."

His words make me want to tear my hair out. "Then tell me what it is. I don't understand why you won't let me in." I wish he'd put me out of my misery already.

A silent war wages in his eyes.

His emotional conflict threatens to rip my heart out, but I can't force the information from him. He needs to trust me, and right now he's unwilling to do that.

"There are things you don't know. Things I can't share." Before I can argue, he cuts me off with, "I can't, Sofia! This is the way it needs to be. There's nothing that can be done about it."

A shield falls over his eyes. The battle that had raged in his gaze vanishes. "If you can't accept that, then we need to end this right now."

Tears sting the back of my eyes, but I hold them in. I don't want him to see that the hope I'd had for him to open up and let me in has been replaced by heartache and sadness. I shrug as if the conversation isn't important. "Consider the matter dropped."

Roman's façade drops as emotion flickers across his face. "I don't want to hurt you."

"You're not," I say as nonchalantly as possible, pulling my lips into a small smile. I'm lying, of course. It feels like a knife has been plunged into my heart.

He scrutinizes my face and scrubs a hand over his head. "I knew this was a mistake. Maybe it would be best for both of us to end things sooner rather than later. Neither of us can afford to get in any deeper."

My heart spasms. It takes supreme effort to keep my expression neutral. I don't want to lose him before I figure out what he's keeping from me.

Until Roman took me in his arms, I didn't realize how empty and alone I'd felt. I feel lighter, brighter, and more alive than ever before when I'm with him.

It's as if my life has been painted in vibrant and spectacular color. The idea of going back to dull, drab browns and grays of the past makes me feel panicky.

The relationship I have with Roman feels like water leaking through my hand. No matter how hard I squeeze my fingers together, liquid continues to seep through the cracks. The realization that I can't hold on to him if he doesn't want me to is a bitter pill to swallow, but it's an undeniable reality.

Instead of giving him the desperate denial poised on my tongue, I take a deep breath and slowly let it out. I calmly ask, "Is that what you want?"

His eyes close for a few seconds and open to reveal a new struggle being fought inside him. "No, it's not. But our involvement complicates matters. I shouldn't have allowed it to happen."

"So you've mentioned," I say dryly.

He turns toward the picture window overlooking the street. His biceps bulge when he clasps both hands behind his neck. Tension radiates off him in thick, suffocating waves. "It would be so much easier if you just walked away."

I stand and walk over to him, looping my arms around his middle until my chest flattens against his back. "I'm not going to do that. If you want to end this, go ahead. But don't ask me to pull the trigger. I can't." Closing my eyes, I lean into him.

His shoulders slump in defeat. He laughs, but there isn't a trace of humor in it. "If I told you everything, Sofia, you would run from me and never look back."

My mind conjures up the worst-case scenarios that would be a deal breaker for me. Roman being a stone-cold killer with no remorse. Him working for the Russians. Him being a rat who has infiltrated the Valentinis close-knit ranks.

My belly pinches with unease at the last disturbing thought. I Immediately push it aside because Roman has been nothing but loyal to my family. He's worked for them for more than five years. My father trusts him implicitly.

But what if he *did* work for the enemy? Would that be enough to make me run from him? Would that be enough to kill my feelings for him?

The man who held me captive with cold steel pressed against my throat intrudes on my thoughts. The way he touched me, the threats he whispered in my ear...

I tamp down the shudder that wants to slide through me and force the memory away.

Roman can't work for the Russians.

Because if he did...

I would have no choice but to run.

CHAPTER TWENTY-FOUR

A bell trills overhead as I push through the door of a high-end bridal boutique on Michigan Avenue.

Grace officially begins her search for the perfect wedding gown today, and my head swims with the reality that her relationship with Matteo has progressed at breakneck speed.

A year ago, my brother hit the town every night of the week with a different beautiful woman hanging off his arm. He wasn't the least bit interested in settling down with one specific female.

He avoided intimate relationships altogether. That changed the moment Grace became a part of his life. I guess what they say is true—when you meet the right person, you just know. Love has the power to change your entire world.

It saddens me that even though I have those same emotions for Roman, there doesn't seem to be a way for us to make our relationship work. I've tried breaking down his resistance, but he continues to hold steady. There's nothing more for me to do but accept the cold, hard reality that the relationship Roman and I have will eventually end.

That thought is so painful that it leaves me gasping for air. I sweep it from my mind to numb the ache and focus on the reason I'm at this boutique at ten o'clock on a Saturday morning. I focus on the joy of helping Grace choose a beautiful gown for her impending nuptials to my brother.

My mother is already camped out on a sleek white couch in the viewing area at the back of the store, leisurely flipping through a bridal magazine.

"Morning, Mama." Tucking all thoughts of Roman into the back of my mind where they belong, I give her a cheerful smile. The last thing I need is for her to catch a whiff of what's going on. The woman is tenacious and will drag the information from me in a matter of minutes.

Then I'll never hear the end of it.

Setting the magazine on the glass and chrome coffee table, she rushes over to greet me. "Hello, darling!" She enfolds me in her arms and crushes me to her as if she hasn't seen me in years instead of a little over a week.

Because I'm hurting, I allow myself to sink into her warm embrace and savor the comfort of her strong arms. We've always been close. In the past, she was the first person I sought out when I had a problem.

I imagined growing up to be just like my mother when I was little. She was always such a strong force to be reckoned with. Although my father presides over the family business, my mother rules the family itself. She's the one we all run to. My parents, despite their traditional values, have always been true partners in every sense of the word.

As that thought flits through my head, I realize how much I want that with Roman and how powerless I am to make it happen. I again have to tamp down all my rioting emotions and redirect my attention. Matteo and Grace are getting the happily-ever-after they deserve. I don't think the same will happen for Roman and me, which is painful to admit.

Roman's secret is wedged deeply between us. Until he trusts me enough to let me in, we'll forever be stuck having each other, but not really belonging to one another.

My mother's hands flutter to my face and caress my cheeks as if she has the power to read my thoughts with the stroke of her fingers. I widen my smile in defense as she studies me with narrowed eyes. Mama is the most intuitive person I know. Not much gets past her.

"Is everything all right, Sofia?" she asks, concern coloring her words. "Has something else happened?" Her brows knit together. "Your father tells me nothing."

Not wanting her to worry needlessly, I shake my head. "Nope, it's all good."

Tilting her head to the side, her gaze continues to probe mine. "How is it with Roman at the house?"

"It's fine. There are no problems." I give her a careless shrug to throw her off the scent.

But she's much too clever for her own good, and follows up with, "Are you two getting along any better?"

I roll my eyes. "We're fine, Mama. Roman is Roman, just like he's always been. We don't spend much time together. I'm at school most of the day and only see him in the evenings." I feel bad for lying, but I can't tell her that he sleeps in my bed every night. If she continues her interrogation, she'll see through my paper-thin façade and everything festering inside will pour out in a torrent.

She makes a clicking sound with her tongue. "Sofia?"

I blink back to our conversation. "Yes, Mama?"

"I'm not sure what's going on, but you don't seem like yourself this morning. If something's bothering you, tell me." She pauses, giving me ample time to jump in and spill my guts.

It's a tried-and-true tactic. When I was a teenager, I would usually implicate myself for any committed infractions. All my mother or father had to do was silently stare at me for about three minutes, and I'd sweat bullets before folding like a house of cards.

To a certain extent, I'm still like that.

I keep my lips firmly pressed together. As much as I want to confide in her, I need to go it alone. "I told you before, everything is fine. It's been a long week. I'm tired."

She pats my cheek affectionately. "You work too hard."

I glance around the elegant shop, taking in the mirrored tables, crystal chandeliers, and mannequins dressed in the latest designs. I need to change the subject before Mama begins discussing my dating situation or the grandbabies she's not-so-patiently waiting for. "Has Grace arrived yet?"

"They've already whisked her away to a fitting room to try on the first gown. I'm sure she'll be out shortly."

We sit on the couch as a saleswoman in a fitted suit, her hair pulled back into a tight chignon, offers us flutes of champagne from a gleaming silver platter.

A second, older woman dressed similarly comes out of the fitting room clapping her hands. "Ladies! Are we ready? I think you'll both agree that Grace looks absolutely stunning in this Badgley Mischka gown."

My mother and I turn as Grace joins us in the main salon. Mama gasps, her hands flying to her mouth. And it's easy to see why. Grace is a vision in a strapless, blush-colored ball gown with a gathered bodice and dramatic ruffled skirt. The saleswoman spreads out the cathedral-length train around her. Grace's blond hair has been swept up high with a few curls left to frame her face.

Tears sting my eyes. "You look like you've just stepped out of a fairytale."

The smile on her face grows impossibly wide. Her cheeks look like they might burst.

I glance over at my mother, who has yet to say a word. Wetness shines in her eyes as she stares at her future daughter-in-law. I slip my fingers into her hand and give a little squeeze as Grace gathers up her train so she can twirl in front of the three-paneled mirror.

"I know this is the first dress you've tried on this morning, but I can't imagine anything else fitting you more perfectly," Mama says, her voice thick with emotion. "You look like an angel."

"We've picked out three others for her to try on," the saleswoman chimes in. "A bride rarely finds her dream gown the first time around, but I have to agree that this one may be a winner. We'll try on the others, just to be sure."

Looking dazed, Mama nods. "Of course."

With the help of the staff, Grace returns to the fitting room to try on the next dress.

I take a sip of champagne. My stomach convulses when the fizzy liquid hits it. I set the flute on the end table and sand as the two pieces of lightly buttered toast I ate this morning revolt.

"Sofia? What's the matter?"

I wave off Mama's concern. "I'm going to use the restroom."

"You look pale." She frowns. "Are you feeling all right?"

"I'm fine." But I'm not. "I think the champagne just hit me wrong. I'll be back in a few minutes."

With that, I dash to the restroom around the corner. By the time I get inside, I'm so queasy that I'm worried I might vomit. I rack my brain for an explanation.

Did I eat something funky?

Do I have food poisoning?

Or is this the flu?

I work in a school where bugs and viruses are always floating around. Last year, it seemed like I caught something every other week. My immune system has improved this year, and I've been healthier.

I stagger to the sink, gripping the edge with both hands while hanging my head. I close my eyes and focus on drawing fresh air into my lungs. It takes a few minutes for the nausea to subside. Once it does, I glance in the mirror and notice that my mother was right—I look ghastly. I splash cool water on my face and reapply lipstick and blush to add some color.

"Feeling better?" Mama asks when I return to the showroom.

"Much." I sit on the other end of the couch, leaving room between us. I don't want to get too close in case I've come down with an illness. "I'm not sure what that was about, but it seems to have passed."

She reaches over and squeezes my hand. "Good. I'm glad you could join us this morning."

"I wouldn't have missed it, Mama." Grace is like a sister to me, and I'm honored to be part of this special day.

My mother gives me a wink and thrusts a glossy magazine into my hands. "It's never too early to start thinking about your bridesmaid dress." She points to a girl on the page. "I was thinking about something along these lines."

I groan and sink into the cushions.

CHAPTER TWENTY-FIVE

A wheel on the shopping cart squeaks as I roll down the cereal aisle.

From beneath my lashes, I sneak a glance at Roman as he walks next to me. Memories of the last time we were in the grocery store together flit through my head. That was almost three weeks ago, and our relationship couldn't be more different.

I pluck a box of Honey Nut Cheerios from a shelf and hold it up. "We ran out this morning." I give it a little shake after a few beats of silence. "You like these, right?" Getting an answer out of him is like pulling teeth sometimes.

His lips lift into an expression that could almost pass for a smile. "Yes, I like them."

I drop the box into the cart and roll my eyes. "Was that so difficult?"

"Extremely."

I grab a small box of Grapenuts from the top shelf.

A month ago, I ate bowls of the crunchy cereal for dinner. I haven't done that since Roman began staying at the house. As I'm about to toss it in with the other groceries, I hesitate. Holding this box makes me realize how lonely my existence was before Roman came into it.

Even when I put myself out there and dated other men, I kept my distance. It was never a conscious decision on my part, but there's no way to be your most authentic self when you're hiding vital parts of your life from the person you're trying to get close to. I self-sabotaged from the get-go and never understood the rut I'd fallen into, in which I bailed once my relationships hit a certain level of intimacy.

No wonder I ate bowls of cereal alone at night while sitting on my kitchen counter.

I used my mother's maiden name when I left for college to separate myself from the Chicago mafia because I wanted people to see me for *me* instead of a Valentini. But all I did was isolate myself from them because I couldn't risk having my real identity exposed.

It's different with Roman, though. I'm free to be me with him because he knows *everything* about my family. This is the first adult relationship I've been in where there are no false pretenses, and it's more liberating than I ever imagined.

The irony is that the shoe is now on the other foot. It's frustrating to have someone continuously holding back a piece of themselves when all you want is to delve deeper, to continue moving forward. But that's an impossibility when there are secrets underfoot.

I'm experiencing what the men I dated felt. Roman is withholding the truth from me just as I did to them.

Shaking my head to clear it, I put the Grapenuts back on the shelf.

Good Lord, who would have thought a person could have an epiphany in the cereal aisle? I want to laugh, but there's nothing amusing about the situation.

"I thought you wanted that?" Roman gestures at the box I just replaced.

I shake my head. *No, I don't want* that *at all.* "Nope." I smile. "I'm going to give Honey Nut Cheerios a try."

He raises his brows in confusion, which is fine. For the first time in years, I understand what needs to be done.

"Oh," I snap my fingers, "I forgot to pick up tea."

"You stay with the cart. I'll go back and get it." He turns and heads in the opposite direction.

I call after him, "Decaf, please!"

He waves a hand and disappears around the corner.

Continuing to push the cart, I throw in a box of chocolate chip granola bars to restock the snack supply I keep in my desk at work for when I can't take a lunch break. Two boys wearing soccer jerseys barrel around the corner and nearly plow into my cart while I examine a selection of dried fruit. They skid to a halt, shout out quick apologies, and race up the aisle. I watch in amusement as they laugh and pull at each other's shirts to slow one another. They look to be about ten years old. Their antics remind me of my brothers when they were younger. My mother spent a lot of time knocking their heads together before separating them.

A blonde woman flies around the same corner a few seconds later. "Jacob! Logan! Get back here immediately!"

I've seen that murderous look enough times to know that if she gets her hands on them, she'll go Teresa Valentini all over their butts. I press my lips together to suppress my smile. I highly doubt this woman would appreciate the humor I feel at her expense.

She shoots me a harried expression. "I'm so sorry! You'd think running around on a soccer field for an hour would wear them out."

I smile in understanding. "I wish I had a tenth of their energy. You need to find a way to bottle and sell it. You'd make millions."

The lines of tension bracketing her mouth disappear as she chuckles. "Yeah, that's exactly what my husband says."

I really could use some of the boys' boundless energy right now. I've been more tired than usual lately. I've chalked it up to my extracurricular activities with Roman.

"I'd get so much more accomplished during the day if I had that kind of stamina," I joke.

She snorts. "Wouldn't we all?"

Roman rounds the corner with a box of tea clutched in his hand.

The woman has her back turned toward him and glances over her shoulder when she hears his footsteps. Her jovial expression morphs into one of shock. *"Roman?"*

CHAPTER TWENTY-SIX

Roman's footsteps stall, his eyes darting from the blonde to me and then back again.

Is this woman an ex-girlfriend?

"MaryAnn," he says tightly. "Hi."

Surprise transforms into delight on MaryAnn's pretty face, laughter bubbling from her lips. "Ah, hi yourself, stranger! I was just telling Gabe the other day that we haven't seen you in months. Where've you been hiding? You must be working crazy hours again."

My gaze bounces between the pair as she chatters away, oblivious to Roman's silence. His discomfort is palpable. By the way she throws names out, it seems like she knows him well. But I don't get the feeling that they were ever a couple. There's a connection between them, but no romantic vibe.

"That reminds me," she jabs a finger at him, "You never got back to us about the birthday party next weekend. Are you going to swing by?"

His jaw locks. "Umm..."

She shakes the same finger with more purpose. "No excuses this time! You'd better come! This is your godson we're talking about."

Roman winces.

"Everyone's going to be there. It'll be a packed house." Glancing down the aisle, she waves at the two boys now arguing over a box of cereal. "Jacob, Logan, look who's here! It's Uncle Roman."

Uncle Roman?

I raise my brows at Roman, who studiously avoids my gaze.

MaryAnn, who must be his sister or sister-in-law, turns and faces me again. "Oh, I'm sorry!" She gives Roman an expectant look. When he says nothing, she huffs out a breath and smiles, thrusting her hand toward me. "Apparently Roman isn't going to bother introducing us. I'm MaryAnn, his sister-in-law, and the two hellions that ran past are my boys. The taller one is Jacob, and the other is Logan."

"Sofia." I take hold of her hand. "It's nice to meet you."

Dozens of questions swirl through my head. I glance at Roman and find his eyes already on me. A strange guardedness I've seen countless times before lurks in them.

The boys run back down the aisle and hurtle their small bodies at their uncle.

Roman scoops them up into his arms with practiced ease, shaking them until they shriek with uncontrollable laughter. His discomfort dissolves, and his guard drops as he focuses on his nephews with a joyful smile that makes my heart constrict.

The Roman I've become acquainted with over the past three years has always been cold and standoffish. Indifferent. The expression he now wears is something of a contradiction. It's like a beam of sunlight filtering down through dark rain clouds.

Roman catches me watching him. The smile on his face vanishes, the tops of his ears reddening as if he's self-conscious about being observed.

MaryAnn's eyes soften as she watches Roman and the boys. "It's really been too long, Roman. It's impossible to get ahold of you anymore. Don't you know how to return a call or a text?"

As swiftly as his walls tumbled down, they're once again resurrected. It's frightening how easily he's able to revert to his normal standoffish self.

I wish I understood why.

Fresh frustration rises up in me.

"It's been busy." He gives her a hard, penetrating look. One I've been on the receiving end of numerous times before.

The color in her cheeks drains.

Not understanding the silent communication between them, my gaze shifts from Roman to MaryAnn.

What the hell is going on here?

And then it hits me.

MaryAnn *knows*.

She knows Roman's secret and just realized that I'm still in the dark, which is a terrible feeling that makes the pit of my belly churn with nausea.

"Oh. Um, okay." Her eyes drop to the squirming boys in his arms. "Logan and Jacob, we should probably get moving. We have a few more errands to take care of before heading home."

This elicits a long groan from them.

A handful of minutes ago, I would have found their reaction amusing. Now, not so much.

Both boys grouse about missing their uncle as they untangle themselves from him. Roman gives them a subdued smile. MaryAnn shuffles from one foot to the other, avoiding any kind of eye contact. This behavior is telling, considering how friendly she'd acted moments ago.

"It was really nice meeting you, Sofia." She looks like she's on the verge of saying more, but changes her mind as she looks at Roman. "Bye, Roman." MaryAnn hustles away with the boys, beelining to the checkout area.

Confused by the interaction, I watch until they disappear from sight as new questions whirl in my brain. I avert my gaze to Roman and sigh at the closed-off expression on his face because the answers I seek will be met with resistance.

Commandeering the cart, Roman silently wheels it down the aisle.

Even though I shouldn't be surprised by his dismissive behavior, I stare in bewilderment. Does he really think he can sweep what happened under the rug and not say a word about it?

Realizing he's not going to wait, I shake off my stupor and jog to catch up with him. I grab the cart and yank it to a halt. "Are we going to talk about what just happened?"

His eyes narrow. "What's there to talk about?"

I sputter out a laugh and give him an incredulous look. "How about we start with the fact that I didn't even know you had a brother. Or any family, for that matter." After a few seconds of silence, I ask, "Do they live nearby?"

He sighs and bites out, "No, they live in Wheaton. The boys must've had a soccer game in the area. I've never seen them around here before."

I arch my eyebrows, hoping he'll elaborate.

He doesn't.

Roman never talks about himself or his family or the past. That's weird, right? I assumed he wasn't close to them or, like Grace's, they were deceased.

But listening to the way MaryAnn carried on and peppered him with questions—before grasping that she should stop talking—made it clear that she was completely comfortable with Roman. And his nephews were the same way. That wouldn't be the case if they weren't in touch with one another.

What am I missing?

What isn't he telling me?

His tight-lipped silence makes me want to scream, but I know better than to let loose. It won't get me anywhere. In fact, it'll have the opposite effect. He'll take a giant step back. I draw in a deep breath instead, trying to calm my chaotic emotions.

He wants me to drop the subject, but I can't let it go. I just want him to let me in and give me a crumb of information.

When Roman starts pushing the cart again, I reach out and wrap my fingers around his forearm.

He turns and shrugs like it's no big deal. "I have one brother. We don't see each other very often."

"Why not?"

He gives me an irritated look. "Because I work a lot. And so does he. We're both busy with our own lives."

Until my run-in with MaryAnn, I knew nothing personal about this man. The only time I see Roman is in my world. Around my family. At the compound. In my house. Sometimes I forget that he has a life outside of the work he does for the Valentinis. I know zilch about his background. Where was he six years ago? What was he doing? Has he ever been married? Is his past littered with relationships? Does he have any kids?

I almost blanch at that thought.

I don't know. About any of it.

It's as if the man didn't exist before he started working for my father. It's a disturbing thought that makes me shift with unease.

Unable to accept his stoic silence, I push again with, "Where do you live?"

"How about we finish up with our shopping and then," he pauses as a pained expression crosses his face, "if you want, I'll take you there. Okay?"

Astonished by this quick about-face, the ball of nerves rolling around in my gut dissolves. Just a bit. "I'd like that."

"Fine," he mutters, clearly exasperated. "Can we drop this now?"

I walk alongside him as we start moving again. "I'm not going to let you renege."

His lips quirk. "I know."

I smile at the little bit of headway we just made.

Roman agreed to show me where he lives. Sure, I had to strongarm him into doing it, but maybe now that I've pried a few bits of information from him, he'll be more amenable to opening up to me.

I almost snort.

Then again, pigs are more likely to fly before that happens.

CHAPTER TWENTY-SEVEN

I scan Roman's one-bedroom apartment, trying to absorb every minute detail.

He lives in the city near the Loop, about two blocks from the El. We've been here for forty minutes, and I've already heard two trains rumble past.

Roman lurks in front of the door. I get the feeling he wants to give me a quick tour and escort me out. Well, that's not going to happen. It took three weeks to get him to this point, and I'm not about to be rushed now that I'm here.

"I told you there wasn't much to see," he says.

I throw a smile over my shoulder and meander around, looking for anything that will give me insight into who this man is. "It's nice."

He snorts but doesn't argue.

The living room has a small brown leather couch and matching chair crammed into it with an end table wedged between them. A large flat-screen television is attached to the wall across from the seating arrangement. Other than that, the space is bare. No posters or art hang on the stark white walls, and there aren't any framed photographs scattered throughout the room.

Much like Roman, the place is minimalistic. Sparse. Blank.

I wouldn't know this was his home if he hadn't opened the door with a key on his chain because nothing of a personal nature suggests that Roman actually resides here.

I expected...

I don't know what I expected.

More, I guess.

I thought I'd get a better sense of who this man was. I hoped I could gravitate toward *something* and, maybe, if I asked the right questions, he would open up and let me in.

But there's nothing for me to latch onto.

Feeling desperate, I ask, "How long have you lived here?"

"Five years."

Clearly, my plan to learn more about him has backfired. Roman isn't going to loosen up and share anything personal, which saddens me because I don't know what more I can do to earn his trust.

I snap out of my jumbled thoughts when Roman's arms slip around my waist. As soon as he lays hands on me, I melt against him. He tugs me closer until his body protectively envelops mine and nuzzles my neck. A sigh of pleasure falls from my lips.

This, right here, is what I live for.

Voice deep and raspy, he says, "I didn't get a chance to show you the bedroom." He nips my throat with his teeth. "Any interest in checking it out?"

I know a distraction tactic when I hear it.

His hands slip under my T-shirt and delve into the cups of my bra, maneuvering my breasts from their silky confines. He strokes and kneads the softness with skilled fingers. "Are there any other questions that need immediate answering?"

Hmmm?

What?

I can't concentrate when he toys with me like this.

And he damn well knows it.

One hand grazes my belly, gliding under the waistband of my jeans and plunging into my panties. Every thought I'd been trying to desperately hang onto scatters like leaves in a brisk wind when he strums my clit.

"Ummm..."

Roman chuckles. "Yeah, I didn't think so."

I almost whimper in protest when his hands leave my body.

Scooping me up, he carries me into the bedroom. His mouth crashes against mine as my arms twine around his neck. Tangled together, we fall onto the bed, his erection pressing against my core.

My lingering questions can wait until when I'm not so distracted by his lips cruising over my skin and his deft fingers divesting me of my shirt as if he's unwrapping a much-anticipated Christmas gift. For the time being, I allow myself to be swept away by the tide of passion only Roman seems capable of stoking to life in me.

CHAPTER TWENTY-EIGHT

I lay wide awake next to Roman, staring up at the ceiling. I normally find the sound of his deep, even breathing soothing, but my mind is restless and refuses to turn off. Which is odd, because I always sleep better when I'm in his arms.

Maybe it's the continuous sound of trains rolling by the apartment building.

Or the strange bed I'm sleeping in.

Or the fact that I don't know the man I've been sharing my body with.

Maybe it's all of those reasons combined.

Unable to take another moment, I throw the covers off my naked body. I creep out of the room to use the bathroom, closing the door quietly behind me.

When I'm finished, I pause, unsure what to do. Tomorrow is Monday, and I need to be up bright and early for work. Plus, I'll need to stop at my place to change my clothes and fix my hair. If I were smart, I'd head back to the bedroom and get a few hours of sleep.

But I can tell this fidgety feeling isn't going to dissipate. If I were at home, I'd make a cup of tea, grab a book off the shelf, and read for a bit, distracting myself with a good story. But there are no distractions here.

And I'm not about to rifle through Roman's cupboards looking for tea.

Instead of moving toward the bedroom, I gravitate to the unadorned window overlooking the street. I watch traffic zip and whizz past for a few minutes. It may be one in the morning, but the streets teem with energy and movement.

I turn away and glance around the apartment with more scrutiny. Moonlight filters in, illuminating the living room and adjoining kitchen. I can't put my finger on it, but the blankness of this place bothers me.

Every surface is sparkling and fingerprint-free. The typical pile of mail most people have laying around is nowhere to be found. No personal items, such as a pair of shoes or a single photograph are strewn about.

The niggle of unease in my belly quadruples in size and grows into a painful gnaw as I look for something, *anything* that proves Roman really lives here.

I've been in hotel rooms with more personality.

That thought reverberates through me as my eyes land on the desk in the corner. Without thinking, I move in its direction.

Because I need answers.

Answers Roman refuses to give me.

The top of the desk is, like everything else in the apartment, free of debris except for a computer resting on it. Even in the shadowy darkness of the room, I can tell it's an older model. It isn't as sleek as the ones that are now being sold in stores.

Are the drawers inside the desk as barren as everything else?

I suck my lower lip into my mouth and bite down. There's no doubt that I would be livid if someone invaded my privacy by going through my belongings. That alone should be enough to make me back away and retreat to the bedroom.

What I'm considering is wrong, and I damn well know it.

And yet I don't move a muscle.

In the back of my mind, I know there are pieces of Roman's life that don't add up. I've tried everything I can think of to coax him into talking, but he refuses. He hasn't left me a choice in the matter.

I expel a long, slow breath.

No. That's not right. There are always choices to make. And I'm choosing this one of my own free will. With butterflies winging to life in my belly, I glance toward the closed bedroom door and release a shaky breath.

If I'm going to do this, it needs to happen now.

My fingers tremble as I grip the handle on the middle drawer and slide it open. If Roman finds me rummaging through his desk, this fledgling relationship will die as quickly as it flared to life.

But a voice in my head insists that something is amiss. And if the last couple of weeks have taught me anything, it's that I need to pay attention to my instincts. I ignored the warning bells that rang right after Victor Dmitriyev sauntered into my office. That had been a mistake.

When I'm with Roman, I don't feel as though I'm in danger. But my instincts are still trying to warn me that something isn't right and this time, I refuse to push them aside. With nothing more than moonlight, I look down at pens, pencils, paperclips and a blank notepad.

My heart thumps as a mixture of disappointment and relief rushes through my veins. As much as I want to uncover evidence that justifies what I'm doing, I don't want to discover that Roman has been deceiving me. That knowledge would crush me.

Part of me wants to shove the drawer closed and hightail it back to bed. I had a peek inside the desk and found nothing of interest. I should leave it alone. Let it go. Unfortunately, my mind demands I finish this in order to be completely satisfied. I shift to the left side of the desk and open the first drawer. Finding a thin stack of papers, I pick them up and leaf through them.

Utility bills.

The name on them reads *Roman Santori* with this address. I move to the next drawer. My brows slide together in confusion as I stare down at emptiness. I have a desk at home, and it's jam-packed with paper because I don't have a filing cabinet. Roman doesn't have one either.

I go to the right side and tug open the top drawer. Other than a handful of receipts, there isn't anything worthwhile inside. Certainly nothing that validates my snooping. I haven't come across a single thing to rationalize my continued search through his belongings. I should stop this madness. Instead, I finger the handle of the bottom drawer and jerk it open since I've looked through all the others.

At this point, I don't expect to find anything incriminating.

My gaze settles on another sheaf of paper. A cursory glance reveals nothing of importance. But I've combed through the rest of the desk. If I come up empty-handed, I can just accept that Roman is a minimalist who doesn't care about aesthetics.

I have no idea how much time he spends here.

Maybe none at all.

Maybe this apartment is just a place to crash at night and nothing more.

I pick up the papers and thumb through them. As with the previous drawers, there's nothing noteworthy. Nothing to prove that Roman isn't exactly who he claims to be.

How *exactly* did I get to this point?

Where did the paranoia come from?

Sitting back on my heels, I rub my temples and sigh. I allowed Roman's silence to snowball into something it's not, which makes me feel like a jackass. Did I ever consider that he told me there was no future for us because he didn't want to be tied down in a long-term relationship?

The more I think about it, the more that possibility makes sense. He said one little thing and I spun it out of control, thinking there was an actual reason for him not wanting to get involved with me.

God, I'm an idiot.

As I'm about to return the papers to the drawer, I notice a small white square on the bottom of the flat wooden surface. I tug it free. One of the corners sticks and the edge rips off. Flipping it over, I see that it's a photograph. The first one I've seen in this apartment. In the darkness, I make out the faint image of a person. Maybe two. I walk over to the window and tilt the picture until light hits it.

It's a graduation photo.

I squint, realizing with a start that it's a picture of Roman. Only younger. He's shaking a man's hand who is dressed in a uniform. The American flag is prominently displayed in the background.

I frown as a fresh wave of shock crashes over me. What I'm seeing doesn't make sense.

Why—

The light snaps on, and my head jerks up.

CHAPTER TWENTY-NINE

"Sofia?" Roman's gaze drops from mine to the photo in my hand.

I moisten my lips, at a loss for what to say.

"What are you doing?"

"I found a picture of you."

He closes the distance between us in five long strides. Plucking it from my shaking fingers, he gives the photograph a cursory glance. My heart pounds under my breast, the sound echoing in my ears.

"*Where?*" he asks in something that resembles a growl.

I cringe and consider lying but decide there isn't a point because he'll figure out the truth in a matter of moments if he hasn't already. "In your desk, stuck to the bottom of a drawer."

He doesn't ask why I was rummaging through his belongings at one in the morning. We're way past that now.

Through stiff lips, I force out a question of my own. "You were a cop?"

Squaring his shoulders, Roman runs a hand through his hair. "Still am."

My mind flips, trying to make sense out of what he just confirmed. "But you work for my father," I say stupidly.

His gaze turns steely. "Yes."

"You're working undercover," I whisper as understanding dawns.

In that moment, my suspicions—the little things that didn't add up—now make sense. My instincts were correct. Roman *has* been keeping a secret from me. I just never imagined it would be something of this magnitude.

"You've been lying to all of us." My voice strengthens as his deceit comes into focus. "You've been using me."

He makes a grab for me, but I shrink back and scrabble away. He looks torn as to whether he should come after me.

"It isn't like that, Sofia," he insists, raising his hands in a conciliatory gesture. "You asked why I treated you the way I did, remember? This was the reason. From the beginning, I wanted you. Keeping you at a distance was the only recourse I had. It was the only way I could remain detached and get the job done." He inches closer and reaches for me.

I slap his hands away before he can trap me and bolt for the bedroom, sickened by how he's been collecting proof for the City of Chicago to bring down my family and indict my father. I need to get dressed and get the hell out of here. I can't bear to be in the same room with him.

The entire time I've known Roman, all I ever wanted was to be close to him.

Now, the only thing I can think about is getting away from him as quickly as possible.

As I dart past, he snags me around the waist and drags me toward his still-naked body. I scream and swing wildly, trying to land a punch. The sobs building inside me pour out in a deluge. My fists pummel his chest, but it does no good. His strength—a quality I once admired—now works against me.

Roman picks me up and carries me kicking and screaming into the bedroom, slamming the door shut behind us. He tosses me on the bed and climbs on top of me, yanking my arms above my head and pinning me in place with his lower body.

"Get off me!" I scream, not interested in listening to any more lies. I try bucking him off, but he doesn't budge. Tears of frustration, sadness, and fear prick at the backs of my eyelids.

Roman shakes his head. "This is what you wanted, right? The truth. Well, now you're going to hear me out."

Narrowing my eyes, I hiss, "There's nothing you can say that will make what you've done to my family okay. I won't let you twist things around." Inhaling a ragged breath, I force it out and try to calm down. "This is nothing more than an *assignment* to you. Me. My family. The Valentinis. You're working to bring charges against us. That's what this has been about all along. Are you going to deny it?"

When he doesn't respond to the accusations I've hurtled at him, I shriek, "That's why you sought my father out in the first place! So you could work your way up through the organization and worm your way into our lives! You've been gathering evidence this entire time!"

Rage crashes through me, renewing my urge to fight him off. I grit my teeth and lift my elbows off the mattress while twisting my torso from side to side.

Roman tightens his grip on my wrists. "Yes," he bites out harshly, "that's *exactly* what I was doing. I'm an undercover detective working organized crime. I was tasked with the responsibility of gathering evidence to help bring down Enzo and the Valentini crime family."

My eyes widen with shock. Hearing him make such a bold statement without a hint of remorse makes me want to lash out. To cause pain. I shake my head as tears slip from the corners of my eyes.

How could he do this to us?

If I weren't hearing the words from his own lips, I would never believe them. I'd defend Roman as if he were family. That's the way he's been treated by us—*like family*. He's one of my father's most trusted men.

Except... he's not.

He's a traitor who wants to betray us.

That thought slices through my heart like a dagger.

I gather my remaining strength and struggle to free myself, but it's no use. His tight grip doesn't loosen at all. Fresh tears leak from my eyes. I want him to leave me alone so I can lick my wounds in peace.

He brings his face close to mine. "Just hear me out. Give me a chance to explain."

The high-pitched sound that falls from my lips verges on hysteria.

"You're kidding, right? All you've done is lie from day one. Your whole life, as far as I know, is a lie. Why should I believe *anything* you have to say?"

He rests his forehead against mine and stares into my eyes. "I'm sorry, baby. I never set out to fall in love with you, but that's what happened."

That admission feels like crushed glass ground into an open wound. Our entire relationship has been built on deception. I don't know who Roman Santori is.

I turn away so that I don't have to look into his dark eyes. Eyes that seem so earnest. Genuine. Eyes that still manage to pull at my heartstrings even though I don't want them to. "Don't say that," I snap. "Just don't."

I bitterly recall all the times he told me to stay away. I should have heeded his warnings. They were probably the only times Roman was honest with me.

"Sofia, please, just give me a chance to explain," he pleads, his voice low and raw.

I keep my eyes averted and use my only bargaining chip. "If I listen, will you release me?"

"After you hear me out, then yes, I'll let you go." He sighs. "If that's what you still want."

I turn my head to look at him with the most vicious glare I can summon. "It will be," I say calmly. After a moment of silence, I snap, "Can we get on with it? I want to get this over with."

Disappointment seeps into his eyes.

Good.

Roman needs to understand that there's nothing he can say to thaw my frigid heart.

"From the time I was a kid, there was nothing I wanted to be other than a cop. Both my father and uncle were on the Chicago police force for about thirty-five years, just like their old man was before them. It was like the family occupation. After I finished college, I applied to CPD and was accepted. I never bothered to put in an application with any other department because I wanted to work in Chicago. Once I completed my training at the academy, I worked the streets for two

years as a patrolman before making detective. My lieutenant pulled me
into his office a year later and asked if I had any interest in transferring
to the organized crime unit. I jumped at the chance since I'd grown up
listening to stories about the Valentini family. Your father is like a
modern-day Al Capone. Within a year of switching squads, I started
working undercover. I spent months researching the Valentinis by
digging through old articles and records investigating your family in
Italy and chronicling the inception of the mafia and your familial ties
to it. I created a timeline of events that shaped who your family is
today. I can tell you obscure facts about your ancestors that you probably don't even know."

I turn my head and meet his gaze, fascinated by what he's
telling me.

"You have to know that the CPD, along with the FBI, have detec-
tives and agents whose sole jobs are to keep tabs on the Valentinis.
That didn't start with me, and it won't end there either."

I nod stiffly.

Of course, I know that. My father is hauled downtown every so
often and brought up on charges, but there's never enough evidence
for an indictment. Which only makes the DA's office more desperate
to nail anyone in my family. After decades of Enzo Valentini slipping
through their fingers, they're out for blood.

And Roman is a part of their effort.

"I was chosen to infiltrate the organization, get close to your brothers, and make contact with Enzo."

Done listening to him, I lash out with, "When my father finds out
about this, he'll kill you with his bare hands. Nothing you've said has
changed my mind. Do us both a favor and let me go."

He ignores me and continues his story. "I started out with small
jobs, proving myself as I went along. It took two years until I caught
Enzo's attention and was allowed in the same room with him. For
some odd reason, your father took an interest in me. He brought me
into his inner circle and gradually handed over more responsibility and
power."

"Yes," I bite out. "You proved your loyalty and were handsomely
rewarded for it."

Roman exhales a long, slow breath and nods. "I've been working with Enzo and your brothers at the compound ever since. At first, I focused on my mission. I never forgot why I was there. I noted which illegal activities the Valentinis were engaged in and documented anything that could help build a case against Enzo. I periodically reported back to my handler, supplying proof whenever possible."

I seethe, wanting to scream and howl in rage. I'm not oblivious. I've never lived in a bubble. I know my father frequently conducts business deals on the wrong side of the law. I'm the first one to acknowledge that.

It's why I changed my name and distanced myself from the Cosa Nostra.

But that doesn't mean I want to see Papa get sent to prison. He's my father. And he's been a kind, loving one. I'll protect him any way I can.

"Since I've been working at the compound, I've gotten to know your father on a more personal level. Not as Enzo Valentini, the infamous crime boss, but as a man. A husband. A father. A friend. When I prepared to go undercover, I never expected to feel conflicted or guilty about finishing out this assignment. The same with your brothers. They've taken me in, accepted me, and made me a part of their family. They've treated me like one of their own."

Another droplet leaks from the corner of my eye. Yes, that's exactly what my family has done. They made Roman one of their own. And they would fight and die for him.

Roman's eyes pin mine in place. "And then there's you, Sofia. I could have steeled myself against their kindness and kinship and focused on the task at hand if it hadn't been for you."

That makes no sense. He's never been anything but cold and distant with me.

"I don't understand," I mutter.

He chuckles, but it's self-depreciating in nature. "Christ, princess, I knew you'd be the death of me from the moment I laid eyes on you."

I've always hated when he called me that. But now it feels like an endearment instead of an insult.

"You crawled under my skin and inside my head, and I haven't been able to get you out since." He rests his forehead on mine again. "I tried so damn hard to fight the feelings you stirred in me."

I squeeze my eyes shut. I don't want to hear this. I don't want to feel the confusion that's starting to seep in at the edges. This issue, Roman's betrayal, is black and white. When my family finds out, there will be no shades of gray.

My eyes flutter open. "Roman..."

"I know," he whispers. "Trust me, baby, I know. The goal was clear when I began working for your family. But the lines blurred over time, and now, being a cop," he pauses, a stricken expression on his face, "feels like the lie." He shakes his head. "I don't know what I'm doing anymore."

A naked vulnerability I've never seen flashes across his face. It tears me up inside. I'm struck with the urge to wrap my arms around him and hold him tight. To comfort him. To tell him that everything will be all right. But I don't. As much as I long to, I can't. This man has endangered the people I care about most, and that is one transgression I can't forgive.

Fortifying everything inside me, I say, "You need to let me go."

His body stays stretched out over mine, and I fleetingly wonder if he'll allow me to leave or hold me captive indefinitely. But then, one by one, he removes his fingers from my wrists.

Uncomfortable with the intimacy of our position, I whisper, "Please, Roman, you have to let me go. I've listened to everything you had to say." I shake my head. "I'm sorry, but it doesn't make a difference. You betrayed us. What you've done is unforgivable."

His lips hover over mine. He looks ready to kiss me, but instead jerks away and rolls off the bed in one fluid motion.

I sit up and gently massage my wrists.

A bleak light fills his eyes. "I never meant to cause you pain."

He's talking about so much more than my wrists.

"I know."

Maybe I'm a fool, but I want to believe all of Roman's claims. I want to believe that he cares for my father, mother, and brothers.

That he cares about me.

It won't change anything, but I really want to believe that he's conflicted. Confused.

Watching him guardedly, I rise naked from the bed. I need to get dressed and leave. It feels like my heart has been ripped out of my chest and torn to shreds. I've never felt this kind of agony before.

What am I going to tell my parents?

Dread fills me at the thought of breaking this news to them.

My clothes are in a pile on the floor. Other than a bed and dresser, the room is sparse and barren. Just like the entire apartment.

I'm not sure why it matters, but I ask anyway. "Is this really where you live?"

His shoulders fall. "No. I couldn't have anything traceable—"

"To your real life," I finish for him, pain lancing me again.

He nods once.

No longer comfortable with being naked in front of him, I yank my T-shirt over my head and drag my panties up my thighs. My heart twists as another thought takes root. "Santori isn't your last name, is it?"

His eyes flash with sorrow. "No."

Oh my God. Everything about Roman is a carefully constructed lie. I never knew this man at all.

Humiliation over being so easily duped scalds my cheeks. "What is it?"

Glancing away, he drags a hand over his scalp. "Please understand that I can't give you that information."

Tears of frustration fill my eyes as mirthless laughter falls from my lips. "Of course, you can't. No need for honesty at this late stage in the game." I haul my jeans up my thighs, zipping and buttoning them with trembling fingers.

"Can we just sit down and talk about this?" His voice drops. "I know it's a lot to take in, and I'm sorry about that. For everything."

I blink back the tears and shake my head. "No. There's nothing more to say."

Relief rushes through me when he doesn't argue. I'm holding on to my control by a hair. My brain is swimming in everything I've just discovered. Drowning. I can't take any more revelations.

"I'll drive you home." Going to the dresser, he throws on boxers, a shirt, and jeans.

"I'd prefer to call a cab."

He dips his head in acknowledgment. "I'll take care of it. But I'll be behind you the entire way because you still need protection, Sofia."

Right. I almost forgot about the Russians.

This isn't a battle I'm going to wage right now. "Fine." I need to get away from him.

When the cab arrives, we silently descend to the ground floor and head outside. He opens a back door, and I slide inside. There's nothing left to say, and that feels gut-wrenching.

Instead of closing the door, he leans inside and looks me in the eyes. Then his mouth crashes into mine. My lips part under his insistent pressure and his tongue delves into my mouth, stealing both my good sense and willpower in one fell swoop.

The cabbie clears his throat and mutters something under his breath.

I plant my hands on Roman's chest and shove him away. Gasping for breath, my fingers fly to my mouth.

He bends until his face hovers over mine. "I spent three years fighting my feelings for you. You pushed and pushed every step of the way, never giving me a moment of relief. You may not realize it, but you're mine now, princess, and I'll be damned if I let you walk away."

My breath stalls in my lungs.

Moistening my lips, I whisper, "I—I need time to think."

He nods. "I get that there's a lot for you to wrap your head around. And I'm willing to give you the time you need to resign yourself to the situation. But we're not done hashing this out. You and me, we're not over. Not by a long shot."

With those parting words, Roman steps back. He closes the door and raps his knuckles on the roof.

We pull away from the curb and into traffic before I can react.

My mind is a chaotic mess. I have no idea what I'm going to do. If this were anyone else, there wouldn't be a question as to the appropriate course of action. I would call my father immediately and divulge every last detail.

But...

I can't do that.

Because this isn't just anyone. It's Roman.

Roman San—

No.

Not Roman Santori.

I have no idea what his name is. I don't even know if Roman is his first name.

I bury my face in my hands because every second I keep this secret from my family is a moment longer they're in danger.

CHAPTER THIRTY

Groaning, I roll toward the alarm clock and slap it.

My eyelids feel like they've been cemented shut. Prying them open takes a Herculean effort. Unable to force my limbs into action, I lay in bed as memories of yesterday assault me.

Roman is an undercover police officer.

Never in a million years could I have foreseen this. If anything, I'd wondered if he worked for the Russians.

But the police?

The Chicago PD?

No. I feel completely blindsided by the revelation. What am I going to do? Acknowledging what a mess this situation is makes me burrow deeper under the covers, wishing I could stay in bed for the rest of the day. Maybe the next few. I had a difficult time falling asleep after getting home because my mind wouldn't click off. As a result, I feel tired and irritable.

I would love to call in sick, but can't.

Two parent meetings and an IEP are on my agenda for today. These parents have rearranged their schedules to come in and discuss their children's educational needs, which means I have to pull myself together and act like the professional I pride myself on being. I'll figure out what recourse to take with Roman afterward.

It's not a matter of *if* I tell my family about what I've discovered. It's *when*.

When the alarm goes off a second time, I groan, roll out of bed, and get dressed. I trudge into the bathroom and wince after catching a glimpse of myself in the mirror. I look like I've been put through the wringer. Purplish bruises sit under my eyes. My normally olive-toned skin is pasty. Applying makeup helps, but doesn't work miracles.

My gut feels like it's been twisted into a series of complicated knots. I should eat something before heading out the door, but I have no appetite.

Last night's conversation with Roman echoes through my brain. Even after hearing the truth directly from him, I still find it difficult to accept.

Walking into the kitchen, I stifle a scream as I find the man I was just thinking about sitting at the table with two cups of steaming coffee in front of him.

"What are you doing here?" I ask, nowhere near ready to face him yet.

"I was hoping we could talk."

The ever-present attraction that hums between us sparks to life, leaving me even more unsettled.

Roman is a traitor.

My father will more than likely kill him. That thought alone makes my blood turn into ice. As angry as I am with Roman, I don't want him dead.

I shove aside my conflicting feelings and rub my temples to stave off the headache brewing behind them. "I'm sorry, I can't do this with you right now." Exhaustion has my emotions prickling much too close to the surface. I need time to rein them in and settle down.

"Let me drive you to work," he cajoles, "we can talk in the car."

I grimace at the idea of being trapped inside a vehicle with him for fifteen minutes. If anyone's capable of breaking me down, it's this man. I have to protect the tattered pieces of my heart. "No, I don't want to be alone with you."

He slides one of the to-go cups to the middle of the table. He knows I usually start my day off with coffee. Two packets of sugar and a creamer rest on the plastic lid. It doesn't escape me that this is precisely the way I like it.

I've craved his undivided attention for so long. And now that I have it, I feel like I'm going to come right out of my skin. It's laughable.

To keep my hands busy, I add the cream and sugar to my cup. I catch a whiff of freshly roasted beans while lifting it to my lips. It's normally an aroma that I suck in greedily. It wakes me up and puts me in a good mood. This time, however, I'm hit with a wave of intense nausea. Fingers shaking, I set the cup down as my belly pitches and roils.

"Sofia?" Roman's brows beetle together. "What's wrong?"

Inhaling a deep breath, I flatten my hand against my tummy. "Nothing. I'm just not in the mood for coffee this morning."

It wouldn't surprise me in the least if these terrible feelings are the aftereffect of last night's emotional upheaval. Lack of sleep and anxiety can be an unpleasant tonic. Working in the counseling profession, I know better than most the toll stress can take on your body.

"We need to finish discussing our situation at some point," Roman says.

That may be true, but I can't handle an emotionally charged conversation with him this morning. Not before work. And not when I feel so raw.

"You dropped a major bomb on me," I snap. "You have no right to come in here and expect me to have already processed everything in a few short hours. I'm sorry, but I need more time."

"I know." He glances down at his coffee. "I told my superiors weeks ago that I couldn't continue this assignment. They've been working to pull me out. Five years is a long time, *too long* to be undercover."

Grasping the back of a chair, I lower myself down as another stark realization dawns. In a harsh whisper, I accuse, "That's why you put an expiration date on our relationship, isn't it?"

God, I'm such an idiot.

He nods. "Yeah."

A fresh wave of anger hits me. "You were going to disappear without saying a word, weren't you?"

I didn't think it was possible to feel more pissed off and hurt, but the shards of pain stabbing through me prove otherwise. After sleeping in each other's arms and making love all hours of the night the last few weeks, he was going to disappear without so much as a goodbye.

"What else was I supposed to do?" he retorts, aggravation crackling his voice. "You were never meant to discover that I was anyone other than Roman Santori, the guy who worked for your father. We weren't supposed to get involved."

I blink back tears, refusing to let him see how much he's shattered me. "You should have done us both a favor and never given in."

He scrubs a hand over his face. "Don't you think I know that?" he asks in a low, ugly snarl. "Don't you think I fought my feelings every single goddamn day? Every fucking moment was a battle. The last thing I ever wanted to do was hurt you. You have to believe that."

Unable to listen any more, I stand. "I don't know what to believe. I need to get to work."

"I expected you to call Enzo last night." He tilts his head. "Why didn't you?"

I look away.

That's an excellent question. One I've asked myself a million times already. I should have called my father right after getting in the cab.

Papa would have snapped up Roman by now.

Which is precisely why I didn't do anything.

Because I can't sentence the man I love to death.

My shoulders slump as I acknowledge my own truths. This delay doesn't mean I won't tell my family. It just means I haven't placed that call yet. I'd hoped Roman would tell his superiors that his cover had been blown and disappear off the face of the earth.

But he's here, sitting in my kitchen.

Ignoring his question, I ask, "Why did you come back?"

"I told you last night that I wasn't going to leave you." He straightens his shoulders. "I won't go underground."

My already cracked heart shudders. How can I believe anything he says?

Roman has already proven himself to be an adept liar.

I take a step back, then another, until I'm at the doorway leading to the front hall. "That's exactly what you need to do. You need to leave." I gulp and add, "And don't ever return. I can't keep this kind of information a secret from my father. I won't risk the safety of my family."

He stands and remains still. "Sofia, please, just give me some time to figure this shit out. There has to be a way for us to make this work. I'll speak with Enzo—"

I shake my head furiously and take another backward step. "They'll kill you if you stay." Tears splash on my cheeks. "As much as I hate you for all the lies and deceit, I don't want to see that happen." I wipe the wetness away with the back of my hand.

"Sofia—" he pleads, desperation threaded through his voice.

"No! We're on opposite sides of the same damn coin. No matter how much we try, that will never change. Don't you understand?"

The hope shining in his eyes dims. "I'm asking for a day. Two at the most. Just give me that before you do anything rash. My feelings for you were always real."

My knees wobble. I just want to curl up into a tight ball until the pain of his betrayal dissipates. "Please don't make this any harder than it already is."

When he takes a step toward me, I turn and flee to the entryway, where I grab my purse and keys. I race to my car and lock myself inside. As I slide the key in the ignition, Roman pounds a fist on the window.

"Open the damn door, Sofia! Don't leave!" he yells, delivering another blow that makes the glass shake.

I ignore him—which is the hardest thing I've ever done—and shift into reverse. The tires squeal as I peel out of the driveway. Slamming on the brakes, my head smacks the headrest. My heart bangs against my ribcage as I press on the gas, thankful for no oncoming traffic. I keep my eyes trained on the street because I don't want to know if Roman is in pursuit.

If he's smart, he'll tell his lieutenant that he's been made.
If my father or brothers get their hands on him...
He's a dead man.

CHAPTER THIRTY-ONE

Three days have passed since I saw Roman.

I assume he wised up and left town. My heart splinters at the thought of never seeing him again. But there wasn't a choice in the matter. I couldn't live with his death on my conscience.

Since there's a lull between appointments, I grab my lunch from the mini refrigerator in the outer office and bring it to my desk. Ella usually stops by at the end of her study hall period to check in with me, so I want to stick around. I unwrap the roast beef and swiss on rye bread, and my stomach flips as I sink my teeth in. Flinging the sandwich onto the wrapper, I dash to the faculty restroom across the hall.

It's unoccupied, thank God.

I slide the lock into place and make it to the toilet in the nick of time. Everything pours out of me in a violent torrent. After my belly is empty, I dry heave until my eyes water.

Once the spasms ease, I sit on the tile floor and push my back against the wall. I close my eyes and concentrate on my breathing until the cramps subside. With shaky arms and legs, I brace myself against the wall and slowly stand, wobbling to the sink to rinse my mouth and splash cold water on my face.

What the hell was that about?

I'll be the first to admit I haven't felt the greatest lately, but this is the first time I've actually vomited. My body just feels off. I'm more tired than usual, and I've been plagued with random bouts of nausea.

I'm not surprised that all the stress in my life is physically affecting me.

I'm teetering on the edge of a nervous breakdown because I'm constantly on the lookout for Roman and I'm worried about my dad and brothers. I had every intention of driving straight to the compound on Monday evening to tell my parents about Roman.

After work, I sat in the school parking lot for ten minutes knowing what needed to be done, but unable to set the wheels in motion. I needed more time to accept what would happen once I unleashed the truth.

One day turned into two.

Which quickly turned into three.

Now we're on the fourth day, and I'm a nervous wreck with an upset stomach.

I scrutinize my appearance in the mirror to make sure I'm at least semi-presentable. Unfortunately, I look like death warmed over. The best thing I can do at this point is call it a day. I'll let Sherry know I'm taking a few hours of sick time and head home. I can drive over to the compound once I feel better and tell my parents about Roman's deception in person.

Just as I'm shutting down my computer, Ella pokes her head through the open doorway.

"Hey, Ms. B, do you have a few minutes?" She smiles.

"Hi, Ella." I hold my hands up, palms out in a *stay-put* fashion because I don't want her to get sick if I've picked up a virus. "Don't get too close. I'm not feeling very well. I was just about to head home for the afternoon."

Her expression turns sympathetic. "That sucks."

I chuckle. Throwing up at work in the middle of the afternoon sucks big time. "It really does."

"Hopefully whatever you caught will pass quickly. Is it a stomach bug?"

"I think so."

"I bet some Saltine crackers and a glass of ginger ale will help settle your stomach."

I grimace at the thought of putting anything in my mouth. "Maybe."

She laughs. "Yeah... I don't miss morning sickness. I couldn't keep anything down the first couple of months. My mom would make coffee in the morning, and the smell made me gag."

A shiver scampers down my spine. It's the strangest sensation. I blink, refocusing on her. "What did you say?"

Ella steps into my office. "Coffee. I couldn't handle the smell of it during my first trimester. I was constantly nauseous. And tired. I read in one of my pregnancy books that, in the beginning, it's like your body is climbing a mountain every single day. That's why you're so exhaust-ed." She shrugs. "It makes sense, I guess. There were days when I just couldn't get out of bed and make it here by the start of first hour." Scrunching her brows, she cocks her head to the side. "Remember?"

A weak smile lifts the corners of my lips. "Of course, I remember. I'm just glad you feel better now."

"Me, too. Actually, I feel a ton better. The doctor said all the hormones raging through your system cause morning sickness. It can really mess you up for a while. Some women never experience any nausea at all." She gives me a sour look. "I wasn't that lucky."

Her words somersault through my head. "I think I've heard that."

Nausea.

The smell of coffee making her sick.

More tired than usual.

My mind grows fuzzy around the edges as if I'm underwater and don't have enough oxygen to get to the surface.

"Oh!" Ella shakes her head.

I snap back to the present and flinch at the thin film of sweat on my forehead and arms. I really need to go home and lie down.

"I almost forgot why I stopped by!" With a brilliant smile, she waves a piece of paper around. "I got an A on the AP Calc exam! Can you believe it?"

With effort, I sweep my own concerns away and pay attention to the girl in front of me. "That's fantastic! Ella, I'm so proud of you!"

Still grinning, she nods. "It was really hard, and I spent a ton of time reviewing."

"Just a few more weeks," I say encouragingly. "And then you'll be done."

"Yeah." Her smile dims in wattage. "Everyone is talking about how sad it is that high school is almost over, but I don't feel that way. I'll be relieved when all this is behind me."

"I understand why you feel that way. This year hasn't been easy. But you've gotten through it. And you've done well. You need to take pride in that."

"My friends keep saying how excited they are about going away in the fall, living on their own, and doing whatever they want. They get to experience all that freedom." Her expression sobers even more. "It feels like I'm really missing out by living at home. I won't even be starting school in the fall." She inhales a deep breath and blows it out. "I know it's the right thing to do. There's no way I can handle taking classes and having a baby midway through the semester. That would be insane."

"You're right," I agree quietly, "it would be extremely difficult. Which is why the plans you've made are your best option. With the baby due in late October, you'll have a few months to settle into motherhood before the spring semester begins. I still recommend taking two or three classes instead of a full load. Attending college can be an adjustment all on its own. And so is having a baby. You just have to take it one step at a time. Everyone's path is different."

The edges of Ella's lips tip upward. "Thanks, Ms. B. I guess I needed a little bit of a pep talk. I really appreciate you being there for me through all this."

My eyes sting from her gratitude. I have to fight to keep my composure. "You're welcome. You're so smart and talented, Ella. I have high hopes for what you're going to accomplish in life."

The bell rings.

She sighs. "I'd better get going. I don't want to be late for class."

I give her a small wave. "Bye, Ella."

As soon as she's gone, I close the door to my office and lower myself onto a chair. The conversation I just had with Ella swims around in my head. Key words that never meant anything to me now take on new significance.

Nausea.

Exhaustion.

Emotional.

Is it possible that I'm... *pregnant?*

The very idea seems preposterous.

In all the years I've been sexually active, I've never had a pregnancy scare. I've never even been late.

I wince, trying to recall the last time I had my period. I rifle through my purse until I find my phone and open my period tracking app. Shock suffuses me as I realize that I'm two weeks late.

How didn't I notice?

I was so caught up in my budding relationship with Roman that I stopped paying attention to pertinent details I normally wouldn't miss.

If I thought the situation couldn't get any worse, I was wrong.

So very wrong.

CHAPTER THIRTY-TWO

I rush toward my car in the school parking lot with one thing on my mind.

And that's stopping at the pharmacy on the way home to get a pregnancy test.

In my two years as a high school counselor, I've had several girls pop into my office, frightened that they could be pregnant. The first thing I tell them is to talk to their parents because this isn't an issue they should deal with on their own. The second is to take a test. For the most accurate results, I advise them to make an appointment with their family doctor or Planned Parenthood to run blood work and take a urine test. If they aren't comfortable with either of those options, I tell them to pick up a home pregnancy test.

Most of the time, they stop in and tell me their results were negative. We then have a *come-to-Jesus* discussion regarding safe sex practices. Abstinence is the only foolproof method, but that's not a realistic option for many teenagers nowadays. And I get that. We go over the different kinds of birth control available over the counter and by prescription, as well as the fact that using two methods of contraception is most ideal.

Clearly, the situation I now find myself in is chock-full of irony.

I'm still clinging to the possibility that I'm late. After all, pregnancy isn't the only reason why a woman might skip her period. There are thyroid issues, stress, over-exercising…

I snort at the last one.

Over-exercising isn't an issue for me. I'm lucky if I can talk myself into stopping off at the gym twice a week to run on a treadmill. And even that's pushing it most of the time.

Ten minutes later, I steer into the drugstore parking lot. I exit my car with nerves dancing in my belly and head inside, searching the aisles until I find three shelves of pregnancy tests.

I study the single and double-stick options. Just to be safe, I'll buy one with two sticks. Plucking a box from the shelf, I peruse the label and replace it, grabbing another to do the same.

Irritation builds as I try to figure out what makes one test better than the other. And who knew there were so many choices?

I see yet another brand and examine it as well.

Arghhh.

I just need to pick one and get out of here.

"Sofia?" a deep voice asks.

Startled out of my thoughts, I fumble the boxes. I whirl around as they fall to the floor and find Roman standing behind me. My cheeks heat as he bends down and scoops up the packages.

His eyes widen when he sees what he's holding. "You're *pregnant?*"

"I don't know," I rasp around the lump in my throat. "That's what I need to figure out."

He sets two tests on the shelf, holding on to the third. "I think this one will do."

I nod in agreement. "I thought you'd taken my advice and left town."

He gives me a hard stare. "You really thought I'd just pick up and leave you?" He steps closer and slips his fingers under my chin, tilting my face up until only he fills my vision and the universe shrinks to just the two of us. "I told you before that you're mine and I'm not about to let you go. You asked for time to think things over, and that's what I've been trying to give you. Time. A few days to get your head on straight.

Maybe you haven't seen me, but I've been here all along keeping you safe. Protecting you."

Relief rushes through every cell of my body. I may have told him to leave, but that's not what I wanted. It never occurred to me that he was just giving me space.

Roman rests his other hand on my abdomen. "And this child is mine, too." His fingers spread. "I'm not leaving either of you," he vows, his jaw clenched in determination.

"I don't even know for sure if I'm pregnant." Glancing around, I add in a lower voice, "I just realized I'm late today."

He jerks his chin toward the front of the store. "Then we should figure it out, princess." His lips quirk at the nickname.

I walked in here feeling alone and scared that I might be carrying the baby of the man who betrayed my family.

Roman's disloyalty and deception still hurt, and I'm not sure how to get past them. Or if that's even possible. My feelings for him are a thorny tangle of conflicted thoughts and emotions. He could have walked away from me and the situation with my family, but he chose not to. He's here.

I don't have to go through this ordeal alone, which makes all the difference in the world.

With a surge of confidence, I look at him and say, "Okay, let's go."

CHAPTER THIRTY-THREE

I clutch the pregnancy test so tightly that the foil wrapper crackles from the pressure. Now that I'm moments away from peeing on a stick, I'm hesitant to go through with it because I'm frightened of what the results will be.

I could be pregnant with Roman's child.

My gaze travels over to where he sits at the foot of my bed, not looking the least bit concerned. Annoyance builds at his calm and cool appearance. But maybe it's just for show. Maybe he hides his emotions better than me. My thoughts and feelings have always lingered close to the surface.

He stands and lays his hands on my shoulders. "Go take the test. No matter what happens, I'll be right here with you. Everything will be okay."

I tear up from the gentle encouragement and heartfelt promise. Life was already complicated before I realized I might be pregnant.

Now...

I don't want to think about what we'll do if the test is positive. I can't imagine that carrying Roman's child will change my father's course of action when he discovers Roman spent the last five years collecting information on the Valentini organization in order to destroy it.

"How can you say that?" I shiver while thinking about what Papa might do to Roman.

He slides his arms around me and pulls me close. His strength radiates outward, filling me.

I grab hold of him and hang on for dear life.

His lips press against my forehead as his embrace tightens. "I'm not leaving, Sofia. You're mine. We'll deal with your family after we get a result. Let's take it one step at a time, okay?"

I nod, needing to believe what he's telling me. I can't imagine us skating through this ordeal unscathed, and that scares me more than I'm willing to admit. Pregnancy or no pregnancy, I know the consequences will be severe.

Roman knows it, too.

"Go take the test," he says softly, brushing a lock of hair off my cheek.

"Okay." I trudge to the bathroom as if I'm marching to my death. Unfolding the directions, I sit on the toilet seat and scan them. They seem straightforward—open the test, hold it under a stream of urine, set it on a flat surface, and wait three minutes to see if my life has been irrevocably altered.

One pink line means not pregnant. Two means there's a baby on board, a possibility that makes my belly spasm.

Tearing the wrapper, I lift the lid and take care of business. I cover the applicator tip with a plastic cap and set it on the counter afterward. My nerves are stretched impossibly taut, and my palms are a sweaty mess.

I pull myself together and open the door, stepping into my bedroom to find Roman pacing.

He stops when he sees me and arches his brows in question.

"I don't know yet. The results take three minutes."

He straightens his shoulders and nods, shifting his weight from one foot to another.

I'm not sure what to do with myself, and I realize while watching

Roman fidget that neither does he. We're both tiptoeing through this situation.

After a few minutes tick by, Roman gives me a sharp look. "The test should be done by now, right?"

Fear snakes through me.

Oh God, I don't want to know.

The results waiting for us in the bathroom have the potential to change the course of my entire life.

I'm not sure if I'm ready.

Roman and I aren't even in a relationship. I have no idea what we mean to each other. We've yet to work that out. And then there's the fact that everything I knew about him, everything my family knew, is nothing more than a pack of skillfully crafted lies.

How can I have a baby with a man I don't really know?

And can I ever trust him again?

"Sofia?"

I nod as his voice brings me back to the present. "Yes, it should be ready."

With his arm around my waist, we walk into the bathroom.

The shaky breath I just inhaled stays trapped in my lungs as we stare at the plastic stick lying on the counter.

CHAPTER THIRTY-FOUR

A guard waves our car through the gate, and we pull into the wooded grounds of the Valentini compound.

Roman received a text from my father informing him that the Russian threat has been eliminated. I'm no longer in danger, and my security detail has been called off.

It's a relief to have one less issue to worry about.

My hand rests on my stomach as Roman navigates the long driveway. Neither of us said much during the twenty-minute ride. I think we're both in shock. I know I am. I may have suspected this outcome, but was still unprepared for it. I shift on the seat as Roman glances at me and wait for him to start this much-needed conversation.

He doesn't though. He just continues to drive in silence as the test results flash through my brain for the hundredth time.

I'm pregnant.

I'm going to give birth to a tiny human being in less than nine months.

My whole world has just been rocked. There's no going back to the way it used to be. I would be lying if I didn't admit that the idea of a new life growing inside my womb doesn't scare the crap out of me.

I'm terrified.

Roman pulls up to the massive stone mansion and shuts off the engine. Instead of exiting the vehicle, he angles toward me and slips my hand into his, lacing our fingers together. "Look, I know nothing has been resolved between us. If anything, shit's even more messed up than it was before..."

My eyes water.

So much is at stake right now. And the odds of walking away without a scratch are stacked against us.

"But I promise we'll get through this, Sofia." He pauses and continues with, "I'm committed to you. And I'm committed to this baby."

I appreciate his sincerity more than he'll ever know, but no matter how hard I try, I can't picture a future together. "How? How can we get through anything when our relationship has been built on lies?"

"You're right," he admits with a sigh. "I lied to you about who I was and why I was working for your father. But everything is out in the open now. There aren't any more secrets sitting between us. My feelings for you have always been real. We'll figure out a way to deal with the fallout, and then we'll move forward."

Deal with the fallout.

I'm not even sure if that's possible.

"When my father finds out what you've done, he'll kill you." I spasm from head to toe at the thought of Roman receiving a bullet to the brain.

He looks away, staring out the windshield at the house. "I know. There's a lot I need to atone for. Once I'm out, I'll come clean. I'll tell Enzo the truth myself. The process has already been started, but I don't know how long it'll take to officially get off the case." He squeezes my fingers. "Just give me a little more time to sever ties with the department."

I shake my head. "Do you understand what you're asking? I can't keep this kind of information from my family." This secret has already gnawed a hole in my gut.

For all I know, Roman is playing me. I don't want to believe it, but this could all be part of a sting operation. Trusting him when he's already betrayed me feels like a huge leap of faith.

One I'm not sure I can make.

"Forty-eight hours, tops." His dark eyes pierce mine. "That's all I'm asking for."

"I can't deal with any more lies, Roman. All of the truth needs to be out there."

He lays his hand against my belly, cradling the new life in his palm. "I've given you every reason to doubt me. But you were all I could think about for three years, even when I was doing my damnedest to forget you. And now you're carrying my child." Determination flashes in his eyes. "I'm not about to let either of you go."

I want to believe him so badly.

I'm not sure if I can, but I have to try since the pregnancy takes precedence over everything else. "I won't say anything right now, but I can't stay quiet for much longer. I won't jeopardize my family's safety." This decision goes against my better judgment, but this man is worth the risk.

He lifts his hand to my cheek. "Let me make this right."

"I'm not sure you can," I say quietly, knowing my family will view his activity as a betrayal. "You're a rat who snuck in and spied on everyone and everything."

He jerks his head. "I know what I'm up against and what I have to lose."

He doesn't give voice to what we both know is at risk, but the truth hangs like a dark cloud over us.

His life.

I frown, realizing that Roman never incriminated anyone during his employment. It's difficult to believe that he didn't find what he needed after gaining access to the inner sanctum. "In all this time, you never found enough evidence to prosecute my family?"

His earnest expression falters as guilt flits across his face. "When I started out, I kept my eyes open. I photographed and turned over any tidbit of information I found. Any recorded conversations that could be used against your family to help build a case were given to my superiors. You have to understand that this was the kind of assignment that could make my career. It was a once-in-a-lifetime opportunity."

My mouth dries at how he was hell-bent on annihilating the Valentinis.

On tearing us apart.

I'm the first to admit that my family isn't perfect. My brothers, father, grandfathers, great-grandfathers, and cousins have all engaged in illegal activities. It was—and still is—their livelihood. My parents never shielded me from the lifestyle or tried prettying it up to portray it as something it wasn't.

I may not want any part of the family business, but my loyalty is steadfast. I'm a Valentini, and I stand with them no matter what.

"Once I earned Enzo's trust, he brought me to the compound himself and gave me access to the heart of the operation. He opened his home to me and treated me like a son." His eyes drop to his lap.

"He cared about you. He still does. He planned for you to take over since my brothers have no interest," I grate out, unable to hide the fury tinging my voice at how Roman duped my father.

Roman shakes his head and runs a hand over his closely-cut hair. "I know."

His troubled gaze meets mine again, and my heart softens because I can tell he's just as conflicted over the situation as I am.

"This assignment was supposed to be a two-year stint. I was instructed to make connections in the lower ranks and gather intel. Just as I was about to be pulled out, Enzo took an interest in me. No one had managed to make it into the Valentini inner circle before. My lieutenant and the DA decided to let me stay. But the problem is that you can't work undercover indefinitely. The deeper you get entrenched, the more dangerous it becomes. Lines blur and cross. You start identifying with the people who are supposed to be your targets after being around them twenty-four seven for extended periods. When you find yourself in a dicey situation, they're the ones pulling your ass out of harm's way."

A distant look fills his eyes. "It's a real mind fuck. You start questioning your objectives and the goals you're working toward. The life you left behind fades into a memory as the one you submerse yourself in becomes your reality." He gazes at my stomach. "There were times when I chose to turn a blind eye and buried evidence so deep that it would never see the light of day instead of turning it over. I did that not only for Enzo and your family but for you. Because I couldn't bear the thought of you getting hurt. You've done nothing to deserve this mess, but you still got caught in the crosshairs. And I'm sorry for that."

Until now, Roman rarely allowed me to see his emotions. I finally understand why. It's because he spent the last three years hiding his true self from me while pretending to be someone else.

I reach up and stroke the side of his face. "Thank you."

Neither of us can help that we're natural born enemies. I come from a family of criminals. And Roman works for the Chicago Police Department, just as his father and grandfather did before him.

He covers my hand with his free one as I cradle his cheek. Closing his eyes, he sighs. The urge to wrap my arms around him pounds through me as I see the emotional toll the uncertainties we face has taken on him.

"Christ, I knew you'd be my downfall the first time I caught a glimpse of you," he says roughly. "I considered pulling out a dozen times, but couldn't convince myself to walk away. I knew getting involved would only fuck everything up. But this," his eyes open as he gently rubs my abdomen, "this is *our* baby. The circumstances are far from perfect, and there will be hell to pay." He laughs grimly. "Who the fuck knows, maybe I'll have two bullets in the back of my head by next week. But I refuse to go down without a fight. That's a promise, Sofia."

Thick emotion clogs my throat, making it impossible to speak.

I still want him.

I still love him.

And I want the child we created together.

Roman clears his throat. "Before we walk in there, there's one last thing you should know—" He trails off as a car pulls up behind us.

I glance over my shoulder and gasp when I realize it's Matteo and Grace. Not wanting them to see us touching each other so intimately, I jerk out of Roman's grasp.

He mutters a curse as my brother and his fiancée exit their car and locks gazes with me. "You have to trust me, okay?"

Even though I'm still conflicted, I nod and open the door.

My brother greets Roman with a handshake and pulls me in for a hug. Grace and I quickly embrace and walk toward the house.

I overhear Roman ask Matteo, "The threat's been eliminated? The Russians' merchandise turned up?"

"As far as I know, yes," Matteo responds.

Once inside, Matteo and Roman veer off toward my father's office. Grace and I go in search of my mother, who I'm willing to bet is in the kitchen. The thick aroma of lasagna permeates the air.

I inhale appreciatively. Strangely enough, I no longer feel sick. In fact, I'm starving. My mother has a tendency to prepare comfort food whenever there's a family crisis. She's been known to churn out pans of lasagna, alfredo, and rigatoni with homemade meatballs and gravy.

Mama hugs Grace and kisses each cheek. When she opens her arms for me, I step forward without a second thought. If there was ever a time I needed my mother, it's now. She squeezes me tightly, holding me longer than usual. She presses her lips to my cheeks, muttering a string of words in Italian that are difficult to decipher.

I pull back and search her face. "Mama, what's wrong?" I only found out about the baby an hour ago. There's no way she can know about it yet.

She shakes her head, quickly turning to the oven to check the lasagna. A pot of meatballs and gravy simmers away on the stove as she flutters around the kitchen, twisting her fingers in the hem of her apron.

I'm so hungry that my belly grumbles.

Grace takes a seat at the table, her eyes ping-ponging between us. Something is off, and Matteo's bride-to-be feels it as well.

Unease skitters down my spine. "Mama, what's going on?" I hardly ever see her this agitated.

Spinning toward me, she closes the distance in six quick steps and envelops me in her arms again. This hug feels different though. It's as tight as a boa constrictor's grip.

I shoot Grace a questioning look over my mother's shoulder, but the other woman shrugs in response.

"I'm just relieved that you're okay." Mama tucks a lock of hair behind my ear and pats my shoulder.

I frown in confusion. "Why wouldn't I be?" Is she referring to the Russian situation? I can't imagine my father hasn't kept her up-to-date with the recent developments. "Roman never let me out of his sight, Mama. I was perfectly safe the entire time."

Instead of softening with relief, her expression turns murderous. Her dark eyes fill with a mixture of contempt and disgust. She glances toward the wing my father's office is located in. "That man will no longer be working for us."

My throat closes. "What are you talking about?"

She shoots a nasty glare at the hallway. "He's a traitor."

"Roman?" I breathe.

"Don't ever say that man's name in this house again!" she snaps, drawing herself up to her full height.

I thought we had time to make a plan before talking to my father. But we don't. Somehow, they've discovered that Roman is a cop.

A wave of dizziness washes over me, threatening to suck me under. I fight off the wooziness and ask, "What are they going to do?"

"That's not for you or me to worry about, Sofia." She gives me an unsympathetic look. "He'll be dealt with."

No.

I can't allow that to happen.

I frantically run down the dimly lit hallway. With a belly full of dread and a heart that feels like it might explode in my chest, I arrive at my father's closed door and fling it open, praying I'm not too late.

What Roman did—using goodwill and friendship to his advantage —is the worst kind of betrayal. I know what my father and brothers are capable of when they're angry. Roman will be severely punished.

Feet grinding to a halt, I take in the scene in front of me and gasp.

My brothers, Niko and Matteo, hold a limp Roman up as Giovanni delivers blow after blow to his face. Roman is slumped in their arms.

Is he unconscious or have they already beaten him to death?

Everything in me stills. All I see is Roman, the man I've loved for years. The father of my child. Yes, I'm still riddled with pain from his deception. But I can't imagine not loving him. And I can't imagine raising this child without him. Just like he said, we can figure out how to work through our differences. We can make it to the other side.

If my family will give us the chance.

My father roars, "What the hell are you doing in here, Sofia? Get out!"

I tremble from being addressed with so much fury but straighten my shoulders in preparation for battle when I hear Roman's labored breathing. I have to fight for him. I have to fight so that our child doesn't grow up with only one parent.

Roman struggles to lift his head, blinking slowly as he focuses on me through blackened eyes. A stream of blood runs from his nose.

I've never condoned violence, so this sight breaks my heart.

"Sofia," Matteo says softly. "You shouldn't be here."

"He lied to all of us," Giovanni, my middle brother, snaps. He has a cool, calculating air about him and is impervious to the violence of the organized crime world. If he weren't running his own businesses, he could step into my father's shoes and easily mete out necessary punishments. "He's a traitor." Giovanni delivers another jab that makes Roman grunt as his head rocks back.

"Please stop!" I beg. "Don't hurt him!" Although I'm scared to death, I meet their gazes one by one and tell the truth. "I know what he is."

Stunned silence greets my admission as they stare at me in disbelief. It feels like the air has been sucked out of the room.

My father regains his composure first and bellows, "What?"

Standing straight, I try not to squirm under Papa's ruthless glare. "Roman told me a few days ago that he's a police detective working undercover."

His eyes bulge in their sockets. "And you said nothing? You didn't think that was something I might want to know about immediately? You didn't think it was important to share with the family that a rat had crawled into our ranks?"

"Please, Sofia, stay out of this," Roman mumbles through a split lip.

I almost laugh at his request. No way can I just stand here and let them kill him.

Giovanni plows his battered fist into Roman's gut without warning.

Roman groans and folds in on himself, but my other two brothers keep him on his feet.

"Shut the hell up," Giovanni growls. "No one's talking to you, rat!"

My father doesn't spare Roman a single glance. His furious gaze never leaves me. The weight of it is heavy. Suffocating. If I didn't feel as strongly about Roman as I do, I don't think I could continue openly defying my family. Papa has never regarded me with so much hostility.

It hurts.

But Roman and the baby are worth it.

"I should have been the first person you came to with this information!" His fist crashes into the gleaming surface of his desk, his face an ugly mottled purple. "How could you turn on your family?"

I have to do something before they beat Roman to death right in front of me. I'm not keen on dropping another bomb so soon, but desperate times call for desperate measures.

Praying I don't make matters worse, I flatten my hand across my lower abdomen and look my father straight in the eye. "Because I'm carrying his child, Papa."

CHAPTER THIRTY-FIVE

No one moves a muscle, and the room is so quiet that you could hear a pin drop.

The spell is broken when Giovanni yanks back his arm and lands another savage punch to Roman's gut. "That's for knocking up my sister, asshole!" he snarls.

I scream and rush forward, wrapping my arms around Roman. "Giovanni, stop! Don't touch him again! Roman didn't do anything I didn't want him to do."

Matteo and Niko grimace, tempting me to punch both of them.

"Let him go!" I order.

Surprisingly, my brothers release Roman right away.

Roman leans against me, trying to hold himself upright so as not to appear weak in front of my family. We stagger toward a leather armchair, and he slowly lowers himself onto it. The swelling and bruises have worsened in the last few minutes. His right eye is almost fused shut and a rainbow of streaks color his chin.

As I turn to face my family, my gaze lands on my mother, who I hadn't realized was standing behind me. Grace is there as well, her blue eyes wide as saucers.

"You don't have to do this," Roman mumbles.

I slip my hand into his and rub his knuckles with my thumb. "Yes, I do."

My parents, my brothers, and Grace are all on one side of the room while Roman and I occupy the other. I've never felt so isolated from them. My family has always stood together. That's what we do. The Valentinis present a united front to anyone who tries to harm us.

And I'm breaking that code by defying them.

Is this man worth it?

Is he worth the strife my insubordination will cause with my family?

I look down and meet his eyes. A wave of love encompasses me, dissolving my lingering doubts as we stare at each other.

I love Roman.

Even if I weren't carrying his child, I would still stand by him and fight.

With solidified resolve, I shift my attention to my family. "Roman is the father of my baby. I've loved him for three years, and I refuse to lose him now."

"Not only did he betray *us*," my father stabs a finger in my direction and growls, "he betrayed *you*!"

I bow my head in acknowledgment. Nothing I say will change those facts. I understand my father's anger because I felt it myself when I learned the truth about Roman. "Yes, he did."

"Regardless of the," a look of discomfort flashes across his face, "*circumstances*, you know what needs to be done. We can't just ignore this violation."

I crumble and tear up in spite of my desire to remain strong. "I know what he did was wrong, Papa. But you can't take away the father of my baby!"

My father huffs in exasperation and mutters a string of Italian profanities. His gaze darts to my mother. Their eyebrows rise and fall as they have a silent conversation. Looking aggravated, my father runs a hand through his thick black hair and breaks eye contact with Mama to focus on me.

"Please," I plead. I'm not above groveling if it will help sway his decision. Nor am I above using the unborn life I'm carrying as leverage. I love Roman. I don't want to go through life without him after everything we've been through. "Don't take him away from me."

A muscle ticks in his clenched jaw. "You don't know what you're asking of me."

"I do, Papa. I know *exactly* what I'm asking. That's how much he means to me." My tongue smudges my dry lips to moisten them. "How did you find out Roman was working undercover?"

"I heard it from an informant in one of the precincts," he bites out with renewed ire.

Okay. I blow out a relieved breath. "No one has to find out about this, Papa. Roman has been trying to get out for weeks. He isn't going to work undercover anymore. He'll find something else to do. A different career."

Papa's narrowed gaze bounces from Roman to me and slides back to Roman. "I brought you into my home, took you in as one of my own, and you stabbed me in the back. You must be delusional to think I'm just going to hand my daughter over to you." He chuckles grimly and adds, "Or this child."

Roman struggles to his feet and draws himself up to his full height. "With all due respect, I'm going to marry your daughter regardless of what you think. Unless you plan on killing me, you don't have a say. I love her. And I love this baby. They're mine, and no one is going to take them from me."

Something deep inside me thrills at his declaration.

My father bares his teeth.

As overjoyed as I am to hear how Roman really feels, the last thing he needs to do is piss my father off while his future hangs in the balance. All Papa has to do is give the word, and Roman's life will be snuffed out.

Roman looks down at me. "Maybe this relationship didn't start the way either one of us intended it to, but you and this baby mean everything to me. I haven't given you much reason to believe in me, but I want the chance to prove myself to you. Give me a chance to show you the kind of man I can be, Sofia. That's all I'm asking for."

I want, more than anything, to believe him. To believe *in* him.

Instead of answering, I glance at my father because he'll be the one who decides Roman's fate as the head of the Valentini family. "Papa?" I ask nervously.

"I have to think about the best way to proceed," he mutters begrudgingly.

Roman lowers his head in respect, aware of the gift he's received.

"You'll stay here until I make a decision," Papa says to me.

I hope no one else in the organization knows Roman's real identity. I'm not sure if my father will issue a pardon if someone does. His pride is at stake. He can't allow anyone to know that the enemy breached us without retribution being doled out.

My father, my brothers, and Grace file out of the office.

Mama pulls me into a long embrace. "You're really expecting his baby?"

As progressive as my parents can be, they're still old-school in some regards. They believe babies should come *after* marriage.

I hate the idea of disappointing them, but I hate the idea of being without Roman more.

"Yes," I reply, hugging her back.

Her lips curve as she shifts her attention to Roman. "Count your blessings that you aren't being carried out of this house in a body bag."

I gasp. "Mama!"

Her eyes stay pinned to the man at my side. "He knows the truth of what I'm saying."

Roman nods in agreement.

Mama moves around me and stands toe-to-toe with Roman, who bows his head in deference even though he towers over her. Her fingers slide under his chin and turn his head from one side to the other so she can take a good look at his bruised and bloodied face. "You were let off easy. Don't make my husband regret his generosity."

"I won't," Roman says gravely.

"I always liked you," she muses. "It's disappointing to realize you spent so many years lying to us."

Regret flashes across his face. "I'm sorry about that, Mrs. V. If I could go back and change it, I would." His gaze dips to me. "But then I wouldn't have met Sofia."

Mama tilts her head to the side, her fingers digging into his chin as she studies him. "If you hurt my darling girl or this grandbaby, there will be nowhere on this earth you can hide that I will not hunt you down."

Roman winces as her fingernails cut into his skin. "I'm asking for the chance to make Sofia happy. I want to give her the life she deserves."

Looking satisfied, her gaze meets mine. "I want what's best for you, Sofia. If you love this man, I'll support you. If you're with him solely because he fathered the child you're carrying, you'll have a difficult time finding happiness."

"I love him, Mama," I say honestly, savoring how good it feels to say those words out loud.

"All right." She sighs. "I'm going to find your father. His ruffled feathers will need soothing." Her steely gaze lands on Roman again. "I wouldn't do anything to draw attention to yourself. I'd hate to see you disappear."

Before I can say anything more, she walks out of the room, leaving Roman and me alone.

The adrenaline spike from earlier quickly dissipates, making me feel as limp as a noodle.

Roman lets out a long exhale and glances at me. "Are you okay?"

I open my mouth to tell him I'm fine, but a giggle escapes.

Am I okay?

His brows pinch together.

The man has been beaten bloody and can barely stand on his own two feet, but he is asking if *I'm* okay?

Tears roll down my cheeks as I laugh uncontrollably.

Oh God, I'm losing my mind.

Roman sifts his fingers through my hair. "Sofia?"

My laughter turns into noisy sobs, and he tries to comfort me by whispering words too low for me to understand in my hysterical state.

When the crying subsides, I sniffle. "I thought I was going to lose you. I was so sure that nothing I said would make a difference to my father."

"I'm sorry for ever putting you in this position. I never intended to come between you and your family. The best I can say is that it's over.

Your family knows everything, and I'm still alive." He leans back enough to look into my eyes. "That has to mean something, right?

I nod in agreement.

Thank God everything is out in the open. There are no more secrets between us. We can truly move forward now. Roman and I and the child we've conceived can all move forward.

He gently brushes my hair off my forehead and touches his lips to mine. "I love you, Sofia." After a pause, he continues. "I don't ever want you doubting me or what I feel for you. Our relationship has been complicated from the start, and I'm sorry for that. Sorry for the lies and the deceit. I wish it had unfolded differently between us."

I consider what he just said.

Do I wish our relationship had been easier? Less complicated? More traditional?

I shake my head. "I'm glad everything happened the way it did. This is our story, Roman. I wouldn't trade any of it for something easier." So much love floods me that I feel ready to burst. "I love you. I've always loved you. Even when you were a jackass. And even when I tried to move on and forget about you. My heart wouldn't allow me to do it."

His lips quirk.

I rarely see Roman smile, which makes it all the more special when he does. I hope I'll get to see more of them now that we don't have to hide anything from each other.

Roman will never be a happy-go-lucky guy with an affable nature.

It's not part of his DNA.

But I'm okay with that. I wouldn't change a single thing about Roman.

His arms tighten around me. "You know that I'm never letting you go, right?"

Less than three months ago, I couldn't imagine those words tumbling from his lips. Hearing them now makes this moment so much sweeter.

"I don't ever want you to," I tell him, rising on my toes for another kiss.

EPILOGUE

Roman Esposito

Four years later

Sitting in a wicker chair, I watch my three-year-old son race across the rolling green lawn.

Sunshine glints off his dark, unruly curls. He's yet to have his first haircut because Sofia can't convince herself to trim his gorgeous baby locks. His chubby legs move at full throttle. He giggles while chasing the newest addition to our family around the yard, a golden retriever named Tula.

Sofia wanted another female in the house to even out the numbers. Since I can't deny her even the smallest request, I give that woman whatever she wants on a silver platter.

I spent the first three years of our relationship acting like a complete prick, doing whatever I could to drive her away and make her hate me.

I get down on my knees every single day and thank God that it didn't work.

My gaze shifts to my beautiful wife sitting next to me, laughing at the little boy and dog as they play. Filled with a deep contentment I never dreamed possible, I lay my hand on her burgeoning belly. She's six months pregnant with our second child, and my hunch is that this one will be a girl because Sofia seems to be carrying this baby differently.

Well, that's what my mother-in-law tells me. And Teresa is usually scary-right about everything.

The simple act of looking at Sofia makes my heart swell with love for her, our son, and our unborn baby. This woman rocked my entire world. I knew she would change everything the second I saw her, and I wasn't wrong. There was no turning back once I lowered my guard and stopped resisting my attraction for her.

I never imagined Sofia would stick by me after how I fucked up royally by betraying not only her but her family. But that's exactly what she did. She stood up to them and declared her love for me in the most humbling moment of my life.

In hindsight, I understand that we were destined for one another.

This woman is my fucking everything.

And I'll move heaven and earth to make her happy.

Shortly after the meeting in Enzo's office where I almost got beaten to death, I resigned from the Chicago PD and started working for the Valentinis. Enzo was still furious and didn't speak to me for a good six months. The closest we came to conversing was when he muttered something unintelligible in Italian before stalking out of the room. I often thought he was waiting for me to fuck up again so he could wipe me off the face of the planet.

The birth of his grandson, Alessandro, seemed to soften his feelings for me. Sort of. Teresa's, too. It goes without saying that Enzo can be intimidating. He blusters and pounds his fist on his desk. He glowers and threatens to string you up and leave you for dead. Which, trust me, wouldn't be a pleasant way to die.

But Teresa...

That woman is the real deal.

She has the heart of a stone-cold killer. Sure, she's all sweet and loving... until you mess with her family. Then you see a totally different side of her. One that can make a grown man whimper like a baby. She'll reach inside your chest, rip out your heart with her bare hand, and toss your carcass out the back door to feed the dogs before going back to the kitchen to finish off her antipasto platter as if nothing ever happened.

Does my mother-in-law scare the shit out of me?

You bet your damn ass she does. I slept with one eye open for a while, waiting for her to come for me in the dead of night.

Whenever I mention this to Sofia, she rolls her almond-shaped eyes and laughs because she thinks I'm exaggerating. Sofia has a lot of her mother in her. She'll do whatever it takes to protect the ones she loves.

And I've made it my mission in life to do whatever it takes to protect her and our children. If that means working for her father and the family business for the rest of my days, so be it.

I'll do it happily.

I can't picture my life any other way. I can't imagine not holding this woman in my arms every single night and raising our kids together.

Sure, I'd always thought being a cop was the be-all and end-all, but I was wrong. This woman, the one who stood by me through thick and thin, she's all that matters. I told her I would never let her go and I meant every damn word.

This woman is mine.

And I've claimed what's mine.

Demi

"Morning, Demi!" Gary, one of the stadium custodians, calls out with an easy smile and wave as he saunters toward me. "Up and at 'em bright and early this morning, I see."

My heart jackhammers beneath my ribcage from the twenty-minute run as I flash him a grin. "Always!"

"You have a good one! I'll see you tomorrow!"

Since I've already moved past him, I holler over my shoulder, "Same place, same time!"

Even with *The Killers* pumping through my earbuds, I almost hear the deep chuckle that slides from his lips. Our morning greetings are a ritual three years in the making. I've been running through the wide corridor that leads to the stadium football field since I stepped foot on campus freshman year. This will be something I miss when I graduate in the spring. Five days a week, I'm up at six, logging in a four-mile run before returning home, jumping in the shower, and heading off to class.

At this time of the day, the stadium is still relatively quiet, with only a few people wandering the hallways. There's something both serene and eerie about it. I've been here on game days when there are thirty thousand fans packed shoulder to shoulder, rooting on the Western Wildcats football team. Three-fourths of the stadium filled with black and orange is an amazing sight to behold. Football is a religion at Western. Unfortunately, the same can't be said for the women's soccer team. We're lucky if there are a couple of hundred spectators in the stands.

I've come to terms with it.

Sort of.

I keep my gaze trained on the light at the end of the tunnel and push myself faster. As soon as I burst out of the darkness, bright sunlight pours down on me, stroking over the bare skin of my arms and shoulders. It's late August, and summer is still in full swing. A whistle cuts through the silence of the stadium, and my gaze slices to the field. Nick Richards has been head coach of the Wildcats for the last decade. He also happens to be my father.

Two days a week, the guys are up at six in the morning for yoga. Dad is a big believer in flexibility. Even though I'm winded, a smirk lifts the corners of my lips. Watching two-hundred-and-eighty-pound linebackers contort their bodies into Downward-Facing Dog, the Warrior II Pose, and the Cobra is enough to bring a chuckle to my lips. Some of the guys actually like it, but most grumble when they think Dad isn't paying attention. Little do they know that he sees and hears everything.

My father catches sight of me and flashes a quick smile along with a wave in my direction. He has a black ball cap pulled low and aviators covering his eyes. There's a clipboard in one hand as he paces behind the instructor.

When I point to the field, he shakes his head. He might make the guys do yoga, but he refuses to participate. Something about old dogs and new tricks. Every once in a while, I'll tell him that he needs to get out there and set a good example for the team. He usually shoots me a glare in return.

Every Wednesday night, Dad and I get together. Our weekly dinners became a thing when I moved out of the house and into the dorms freshman year. He's busy coaching football, and my schedule is packed tight with school and soccer. Getting together once a week is the best way for us to stay connected. It doesn't matter if we're in the middle of our seasons; we always make time for each other. Especially since Mom lives in sunny California. After eighteen years of marriage, she got fed up with being a distant second to the Western University football program. She packed up her bags and walked out. I hate to say it, but Dad didn't notice her absence for a couple of days. Which only proved her point. Now she's remarried, learning to surf, and is a vegan. I visit for a couple of weeks during the summer before soccer training camp starts up at the end of June.

Even though it's only the two of us, our weekly dinners are set for three people.

I tell myself to stare straight ahead and not glance in his direction.

Don't do it!

Don't you dare do it!

Damn.

My gaze reluctantly zeros in on him like a heat-seeking missile. Long blond hair, bright blue eyes, sun-kissed skin, and muscles for miles. And he's tall, somewhere around six foot three.

I'm describing none other than Rowan Michaels.

Otherwise known as the bane of my existence.

My dad discovered the talented quarterback the summer before we entered high school and took him under his wing. Which has been...aggravating. In the seven years since, Rowan has become an irritatingly permanent fixture in my life. He's the brother I never wanted or asked for. He's the gift I wish I could give back. He's the son my father never had but secretly longed for.

On a campus with over thirty thousand students, one would think that avoidance would be easy to accomplish. That hasn't turned out to be the case. Somehow, we ended up in the same major—Exercise Science. I get stuck in at least one class with the guy each semester. This time it's statistics, which is a requirement. Three times a week, I'm forced to see him. And then there are the weekly dinners at Dad's house.

Every Wednesday, Rowan shows up without fail.

It's so annoying.

No, *he's* annoying!

Our gazes collide, and electricity sizzles through my veins before I immediately snuff it out and pretend it never happened.

I am not attracted to Rowan Michaels.

I am not attracted to Rowan Michaels.

I am not attracted to Rowan Michaels.

Maybe if I repeat the mantra enough times, it'll be true. That's the hope I cling to. I've made it through the last seven years trying to convince myself of this. I only have to get through our final year together, and then we'll go our separate ways—me to graduate school or maybe to the Women's National Soccer League, and Rowan to the NFL. He's one of the most talented quarterbacks in the conference. Hell, probably the country. There is little doubt in my mind that he'll be a first-round draft pick come next spring.

Trust me when I say that Rowan Michaels fever is alive and well at Western University. His fanbase is legendary. The guy is a major player.

Both on and off the field.

Girls fall all over themselves to be with him. They fill the stands at football practice, show up at parties he's rumored to be at, and basically stalk him around campus.

It's a little nauseating. Don't these girls have any self-respect when it comes to a hot guy?

I wince at that unchecked thought.

Fine...I'll begrudgingly admit it; he's good-looking.

I shake my head as if that will banish the insidious thoughts currently invading my brain. Enough about Rowan. It's time to focus on the reason I'm at the stadium at this ungodly hour. I rip my gaze from him as I hit the cement staircase. After half a flight, all thoughts of the blond quarterback vanish from my mind. How could they not when my quads, glutes, and calves are on fire, screaming for mercy as I force myself to the nosebleed section. By the time I finish, my legs are Jell-O, and I still have a two-mile run back to the apartment I share with my best friend off-campus.

I give Dad a half-hearted wave before leaving. It's the most I can muster. His lips quirk at the corners as he shakes his head. He thinks I'm crazy. At the moment, I can't argue with his assessment of the situation. Although, it's the extra training I put in that helps me run circles around the other team in the second half of the game.

The jog home feels like it will last forever. By the time I unlock the apartment door, I'm ready to collapse. I beeline for the shower and jump in before it's fully warm. My skin prickles with goose flesh, but it feels so damn good. Twenty minutes later, I'm dressed and ready to take on the day. My hair has been thrown up in a messy bun, and I'm making a protein smoothie that will fuel me for my morning classes.

Just before taking off, I poke my head into Sydney's room. I know exactly how I'll find her, and that's buried beneath a small mountain of blankets. She doesn't disappoint. We met the summer before freshman year in training camp and have been besties ever since. She's the yin to my yang. The peanut butter to my jelly. The Thelma to my Louise. Where I'm more introverted and cautious, she's loud and boisterous. She's been known to leap without necessarily looking at what she's jumping into. Every so often, it gets us into trouble. Sydney and I have lived together since sophomore year. I gave up trying to cajole her ass out of bed for a six o'clock run after the first week of us cohabitating when she nearly took my head off with an alarm clock.

"It's that time again," I sing-song obnoxiously, "rise and shine."

There's a grunt and then some shifting from under the blankets that tells me she's alive.

When I chant her name repeatedly, each time escalating in volume, she growls, "Get the fuck out!"

"Awww," I mock, "that's so sweet. I love you, too."

Sydney snorts before a hand snakes out from beneath the blankets to give me a one-fingered salute. Then she grabs a pillow and tosses it in my general vicinity. It falls about five feet short of its mark.

I stare at the dismal attempt. "If you're trying to cause bodily harm, you'll have to do better than that."

"Piss off."

"All right then." I shrug. "See you after class." With that, I close the door behind me.

My farewell is met with another indecipherable mouthful. If this weren't something we went through on the daily, I'd worry she was in the midst of a stroke. Sydney is definitely not a morning person. She's more of an early afternoon person. Another thing I've learned over the years? The action of waking up to a brand-new day is a gradual process.

She's like a bear rousing prematurely from hibernation. It's not a pretty sight. She's lucky I don't take her insults personally.

I grab my backpack from the small table crammed into the break-fast nook area along with a coffee before heading out the door. The apartment I share with Sydney is located three blocks from campus, which is highly sought out real estate. We're fortunate Dad is friends with the guy who manages the building. It's probably one of the only perks of having a father who is a head coach of a college football team.

You'd think there would be more, but you'd be wrong. Honestly, being Nick Richard's daughter is more of a hindrance than anything else. People assume you receive special treatment on campus, from professors, or that you have an in with all the football players.

Or worse...

Much worse.

After a bunch of ugly—not to mention untrue—rumors circulated freshman year, I've done my best to distance myself from the Wildcats football team. They're a great bunch of guys, but I don't need all the ugly gossip and speculation that comes along with being friends with them.

As I reach Corbin Hall, the mathematics building for my stats class, my gaze is drawn to a clump of students standing around outside the three-story, red-brick building. In the center of that crowd is Rowan. I don't have to see him physically to know that he's close. The muscles in my belly contract with awareness. It's like a sixth sense. One I wish would go away. He's the last person I want to be cognizant of.

As I jog up the wide stone stairs to the entrance, my gaze fastens on him. A smirk twists the edges of his lips, and my eyes narrow before I drag them away and yank open the door to the building. Relief rushes through me as I step inside the air conditioning and disappear from sight.

"Hey, Demi, wait up!"

I turn at the sound of my name before slowing my step. The dark-haired guy jogging to catch up smiles before falling in line with me.

Justin Fischer.

He's a baseball player and teammates with Sydney's boyfriend,

Ethan. We've been seeing each other for about a month. It's still casual at this point. With school and soccer, I don't have a ton of time to invest in a relationship. He seems to understand that and isn't pushing to be more serious.

When he leans in for a kiss, I angle my head. At the last moment, he tilts in the opposite direction, and we end up bumping teeth instead of locking lips. With a grunt, I pull away and chuckle. My fingers fly to my mouth to make sure I haven't chipped a tooth.

Maybe I've been reluctant to admit it to myself, but that kiss sums up our relationship perfectly.

Awkward and a step out of sync with each other.

"Sorry," he murmurs with a slight smile. I search his face and wait for any telltale sign of sexual chemistry to ping inside me. Unfortunately, my insides remain completely unfazed, which is disappointing but not altogether unexpected. I had a sneaking suspicion when we first got together that it might turn out this way.

"No problem," I say, hoisting my smile and brushing aside those thoughts.

"I haven't seen you for a couple of days," he remarks as we turn a corner and continue walking.

"It's been busy." Which isn't a lie. School might have recently started, but the academics at Western are rigorous. And being a Division I athlete is more like a job. If you're not ready to put in the work, don't bother showing up. There's no half-assing it around this place.

"When's your next game?" he asks.

"Tomorrow at six." My gaze flickers in his direction. Not that I expect him to come, but...

Fine, so maybe I do. If he wants to be my boyfriend, then he needs to show a little support.

His dark brows draw together. "That sucks. I've got a mandatory study hour I have to attend."

I shrug off the disappointment. It's another nail in the coffin of this relationship as far as I'm concerned. "That's cool. It's not a big deal."

"But I'll see you tonight?"

Oh. Right.

Tonight.

Well, damn. In a moment of weakness, I threw out an invitation to join our Wednesday evening dinner. It's one I now regret. If only there were a gracious way to rescind the offer.

"If you're busy, I totally understand—"

"Are you kidding? No way." With a grin, he shakes his head. "I wouldn't miss it for the world. I'm looking forward to meeting Coach Richards."

Great. So this is more about my father than me? Exactly what every girl wants to hear.

I force a brittle smile. "Awesome. He's excited, too."

That might be something of an overstatement.

Justin nods toward the end of the corridor. "I better get moving. Professor Andrews is a real stickler for punctuality."

"Yup. See you later."

This time, when he leans in, our lips align perfectly. The kiss is nothing more than a fleeting caress. There and gone before I can sink into it.

And I'm left feeling...absolutely nothing.

I bury the disappointment where I can't inspect it too closely before giving him a wave as he takes off. For a moment, I stand rooted in the hallway and watch as he disappears through the crowd. There's nothing to distinguish Justin from the thousands of guys who look exactly like him on campus. He's of average height and build with dark hair and espresso-colored eyes. He's nice enough. Although, if I'm completely honest, he's a little self-absorbed. He talks about baseball all the time. If Ethan hadn't introduced us, he's not someone I would have looked twice at. We don't have a ton in common.

As much as I hate to admit it, this relationship has probably reached its expiration date.

Now it's a matter of pulling the plug.

Ugh. I hate breakups. Although, it's doubtful this will end up destroying him. I'll have to make it through tonight and figure out the rest.

With a sigh of resignation, I head to the classroom and find a seat tucked away in the far corner of the small lecture hall. A lanky guy I recognize from a few of my other classes settles beside me. He flashes a dimpled smile as we empty our backpacks.

The tiny hair at the nape of my neck rises seconds before Rowan enters the room. It's like my body knows when he's within a thirty-foot radius. I glance at him from beneath the thick fringe of my lashes before shifting away. Air becomes wedged in my lungs as I wait for him to take a seat. And it won't be next to me because I'm—

"Hey man, would you mind moving?"

Surrounded on both sides.

Damnit. I'm hoping the cutie next to me will tell Rowan to go take a flying leap.

What? It could happen. Not everyone at this university is enamored of the football-playing god. Although I realize the odds aren't stacked in my favor. Rowan is the most recognized athlete on campus. People fall all over themselves to accommodate him.

It's a little sickening.

Okay, maybe more than a little.

"Sure, no problem, Michaels." The guy next to me hastily packs up his books before vacating the desk. Unable to ignore him any longer, I glare as Rowan slides onto the seat next to me.

"Did you really think you could evade me that easily?" Laughter brims in his deep voice. A voice, I might add, that does funny things to my insides.

"One can always hope, right?"

"Oh, answering a question with a question." He leans closer, eating up some of the much-needed distance between us. "I like it."

I roll my eyes as his lips stretch into a satisfied grin. Irritation bubbles up inside me when sexual tension blooms at the bottom of my belly. Or maybe that tension has settled a little lower.

It's definitely lower.

I'm tempted to swear like a sailor. How is it possible that I feel nothing for the guy I'm actually dating, and yet my pulse skitters out of control for someone I don't even like? It's so freaking ironic. It's been this way since we met, and nothing I do stomps it out. I can try to fool myself into believing it's not there, but that doesn't make it any less true.

It's a relief when Professor Peters takes his place at the podium and clears his throat. Once he's captured everyone's attention, he delves headfirst into the probability of dependent and independent events.

Grateful for the excuse to ignore Rowan for the next fifty minutes, I open my textbook and concentrate on the lesson. Just as the blond boy fades into the background, his bare knee bumps into mine. Electricity ricochets through my entire being. I glance at him to see if he's noticed the strange energy we always seem to generate and find his ocean-colored gaze fastened to mine.

My guess is that he does.

Damnation.

ABOUT THE AUTHOR

Jennifer Sucevic is a USA Today bestselling author who has published nineteen New Adult and Mature Young Adult novels. Her work has been translated into German, Dutch, and Italian. Jen has a bachelor's degree in History and a master's degree in Educational Psychology. Both are from the University of Wisconsin-Milwaukee. She started out her career as a high school counselor, which she loved. She lives in the Midwest with her husband, four kids, and a menagerie of animals. If you would like to receive regular updates regarding new releases, please subscribe to her newsletter here- Jennifer Sucevic Newsletter (subscribepage.com)
Or contact Jen through email, at her website, or on Facebook.
sucevicjennifer@gmail.com
Want to join her reader group? Do it here -)
J Sucevic's Book Boyfriends | Facebook
Social media links-
www.jennifersucevic.com
https://www.instagram.com/jennifersucevicauthor
https://www.facebook.com/jennifer.sucevic
Amazon.com: Jennifer Sucevic: Books, Biography, Blog, Audiobooks, Kindle
Jennifer Sucevic Books - BookBub
https://www.tumblr.com/blog/jsucevic
https://www.pinterest.com/jmolitor6/